A demon smiled down at her, barely visible in the darkness – an imposing silhouette against the bed's ornate canopy. His glittering white smile, of course, could not be missed. Nor could his searing orange eyes, broken up by spots of clear, intense blue. The bits of blue were enough to tell her that his demon form had not taken his human one over completely, not yet. But he was hungry. He had come to collect his due.

JASPER BLACK

A Chamber Press Book

Swallow You Whole
Copyright © 2015 by Jasper Black

www.chamber-press.com

Book design by Leanna Teneycke

First paperback edition, 2016

Chamber Press

Swallow You Whole

PART 1: HELL, INC

CHAPTER 1

It was raining the night Lord Clifton died, and a demon came for his soul.

Lady Clifton sat dutifully by her husband's side. She had been there all day, and would remain with him through the night until they came to take away his body. She watched as her lord's last breath rattled past his cracked lips, dry save for the corners - wet with his own phlegm. A hacking cough sent him to Heaven at last, as if his body had grown weary with living and was trying to vomit up his soul. Frail shoulders sank into his satin pillows, and his accusing eyes had turned to her, bloodshot and burning with hatred. He blamed her. Had every right to. But there was no help for it now, he was as good as dead.

Her smile was soft and serene as she dipped the edge of a rag into a bowl of rose scented water and dabbed the beads of sweat away from his shiny forehead, blazing with fever.

When she pulled her hand away, he was dead, but his eyes were locked on her.

Violet Clifton set the bowl down on the bedside table. Her sigh was relief, interwoven with anxiety. Lord Clifton had not been an old man, and there would be talk for weeks about how it was such a tragedy. A promising young man, a whale oil magnate, a dutiful husband – struck down his prime by dreadful consumption. No one would blame her, but the mourning period would be long; and black, she felt, did not do justice to her clear winter complexion.

Violet extended her hand, placing gentle fingertips against Lord Clifton's heavy eyelids. He had such puppy dog eyes, downturned and deep-set. Bedroom eyes, some would say. They drew you in from across the room, seduced you, promising nothing but pleasure. They brightened in the natural sun but came alive in sultry lighting. And they lied so well, just like his stern, thin lips.

For a moment, she hesitated to close them forever.

Too little, perhaps, too late.

Another hand settled on top of hers, colder than the thin rain that was splattering against the grand windows. Violet closed her eyes and sighed as she felt her hand being weighed down, and Lord Clifton's eyes saw the last of the world he was leaving behind.

"Hesitation," a rich baritone voice whispered against her ear, "is the enemy of anyone who strives to be great."

"It was only a moment." She brushed him away, still unable to pull her eyes away from the dead man in front of her. His face was white like wax. His unusually thick brown hair had gone limp and oily, clinging to his neck and temples and just starting to curl with length. Her lip drew back in a sneer, and she turned her hand over, grasping cold fingers in her warm palm and lifting her head slightly to look up.

A demon smiled down at her, barely visible in the darkness – an imposing silhouette against the bed's ornate canopy. His glittering white smile, of course, could not be missed. Nor could his searing orange eyes, broken up by spots of clear, intense blue. The bits of blue were enough to tell her that his demon form had not taken his human one over completely, not yet. But he was hungry. He had come to collect his due.

He reached out, his free hand lowering to meet the deceased lord's chest. Long, needle-like talons grew from his nails and skittered over Lord Clifton's nightshirt, pausing just above his heart, tugging at the fabric.

"It is there," the demon said, his voice thick with desire. "Sitting just behind the heart. It is trembling. It is afraid."

Lady Violet turned her head. "Go on, then."

He pulled his other hand away from hers, eagerly stepping closer to his prey. The demon set one knee onto the bed, swinging his other leg around so that he was straddling the lord's corpse obscenely. Leaning forward, he hummed softly, talons ripping at the delicate linen of the nightshirt and pulling it open. Bare chest, slick with sweat, growing colder with each passing second.

The demon lowered himself even further. He kissed the lord's throat like a lover while sinking his talons as deep as they could go into the sunken chest. Dead flesh parted, blood pouring sluggishly from the wound. The demon set his teeth and shoved his fingers into the opening, grasping the ribcage and cracking it open with a pop, the sickly sound of bone grinding against bone.

Steam hit his face, and he dipped his hand into the ribcage, parting organs with slender fingers until he found the source of his prize.

The demon wrapped his hand around the heart and wrenched it free, flinging it into Lady Violet's lap. Blood soaked through the front of her dress but she kept her steely gaze fixed forward. Her lips pressed together, she did not look down or say a word.

Lord Clifton's soul was lapped up like cream. The demon made no effort to conceal the satisfied smacks and slurps that accompanied his enjoyment of the meal.

An eternity passed. Eventually, he lifted the heart out of her lap.

"You can look, now," that nice baritone voice said. Lady Violet's eyes fell back to her dead husband, His chest had been pushed back into place, sutured up so that none would know the difference. A fresh nightshirt had been pulled down over his head. She didn't ask what the demon had done with the other.

"It is done," she said, and her voice fell flat.

"Well, it could be." The demon was sitting on the edge of the bed, all smiles and gleaming blue eyes. In the spill of moonlight from the window behind her she could see soft, downy blonde curls; thick, unmanageable, much like her husband's had been.

"Or?" She lifted one dark brow in response to his hanging implication.

"Or you could sign another contract with me," he said, and his grin widened.

She scoffed. "I do not have another soul to give you."

"You have your own. And I'm sure it has a much darker, bitter taste than his." He gestured to the dead lord.

She slid one of her hands over the other, toying nervously with the ring on her wedding finger. "I could still use you," she said thoughtfully. "A woman alone, in this day and age..."

"Verily," he said, standing to move behind her, a cat on the prowl. "Think on it. Banish me back to hell, and I am out of your life forever. But then you will have to take another weak, foolish husband who will manage your previous lord's accounts and try to put more ill-fated children in your belly. Then you are right back where you started. On the other hand." He slid his hands over her shoulders. Under the heavy perfume of cloves, he smelled like blood and rotting meat.

"Sign a contract with me," he said. "I can pose as your husband, and I will serve you. And together, we will seize the monarchy by its throat. We can make you a pivot of society. And I your faithful slave; eyes and ears who will go everywhere, see everything for you. What will it cost you, in the end? A soul. A simple soul." Fingertips, now slightly warm, slid down her cheek. "Many years now, long after you should naturally die. And as you can see..."

He dared to brush his lips over the shell of her ear, "it does not hurt a bit."

He really was first rate. She could feel her heart pounding against her chest. Her soul was protesting, beating its wings against the walls of its prison. Her entire ribcage ached and she choked on her words twice before she could force them out.

"You don't look a thing like him."

He pulled her chin up to face him and he blinked, slowly, as if she had jolted him out of a trance. If one looked closely, they could see all three eyelids gliding at various speeds over his cornflower blue irises.

"Pardon me?" He sounded irate, releasing his hold on her. He brushed his hand through the air as if batting away a bothersome fly.

"You do not look a thing like William." She fussed with her nails, unattractively peeling; the corners bitten to ragged, misshapen edges. People wondered why she was always wearing gloves. "Oh, did you mean to pose as my *new* husband?" She looked up, her eyes flashing – faintly accusatory. "The proper mourning period is at least a year. Then you would have to appear, presenting yourself as an established suitor. In the interim, his every relative will be crawling all over his estate. They will have his business, all he worked for and all I managed behind the scenes, neatly diced up and there will be nothing left for me in the end. I am not going to be at the mercy of his brothers, those oily leeches will probably spend the better part of my mourning year betting against each other for the right to 'court' me. And I will not stand for any of that."

"I see." He slid easily back into his groove, once he knew in which direction the conversation was headed.

"Your despair is wasted, my lady." He took her hand. "I can be anything you like." Even as he spoke, his voice bore a subtle change – developing that faint rasp that William had recently acquired from all of his years sucking on his tobacco pipe. His palms widened, his long fingers shortening and the long, almond shaped nails squared off – neatly trimmed as well. His honeyed skin faded to sickly milk. When she looked at his face again, his hair was dark. His eyes had changed completely – having gone from cornflower blue to burnt umber. Mournful puppy dog eyes… yet bereft of William's somber austerity.

She doubted that Henry – as the demon had named himself– was capable of ever being too serious.

"A remarkable resemblance, don't you find?" he preened. "Not to my taste, certainly. But I am sure it is all the rage for your dull, grey society."

"Mm." Her eyes flickered over him, studying every inch. His height and build was exact. He had gotten everything right to the final detail, including the scar on William's upper lip. "It is very good. Yet… I don't think it is quite worth my soul."

He scowled.

She held up a finger. "I recall another I can harvest for you."

"A bitter one?" he asked hopefully, flopping down on the bed, stretching out next to her dead husband. Side by side, one looked like a waxwork version of the other.

"Even more so than mine," she said.

He was temporarily distracted by pulling on the dead Lord Clifton's bottom lip.

"My sister," she continued, even though he had asked for no explanation, "has a son who I think is quite suited to your tastes. The doctors have given him less than a year to live, anyway."

"A looming cloud of death does tend to make a bitter man." Henry smiled, and ran his tongue over his sharp canines. "If I am to accept your offer, the contract must be signed the same way as the last. A piece of him, and a piece of you – both given willingly."

"It will not be difficult," she said, somewhat dismissively. "I will arrange for a visit with my sister. We will leave in a few days." She looked down at the corpse lying, disheveled, on the bed. "What do we do with him? If you are to take over his identity, we cannot very well send him to an undertaker."

"That much you can leave to me," Henry said, sliding an arm around Lord Clifton's stiff, broad shoulders and dragging the body close as if it were a lover, kissing the top of the dead lord's lolling head. "Bones and all … I assure you that no part of him shall go to waste."

"I am counting on it." She rose. The heart had rested long enough in her lap to soak through every layer, and now the cold blood brushed against her legs with every step, sending shivers up her spine. The entire outfit had been ruined. She would have to have it burned.

She left the room, and shut the door behind her. The wood warped in the frame, sealing off the entrance, and an eerie silence fell – followed by hisses, growls, wet sucking and bones snapping – joints popping and tendons ripping.

She swallowed the bile that rose to her mouth. It burned a path down her throat as she continued down the hall, her stomach tightening in knots.

Rain had been replaced by an impenetrable white curtain of fog, and Elliot called out for a demon.

He sat in front of his window, high enough to look out over most of the estate. Of course, the fog covered most of it, slithering around the garden walls and seeping into the carefully trimmed rosebushes. It crawled over the mansion walls, tickling the wet ivy leaves, and skated over the rippling fountain waters. Over the family cemetery, it rested like a thick grey blanket that had been draped across the slumbering dead. The only thing it did not cover was the fresh grave, a gaping black hole in the earth that they had finished hollowing out only days ago. It yawned before a tall tombstone, half-finished, with a name and a birth date. But nothing else.

Far more unsettling for Elliot than staring at his own grave was the sight of the demon that emerged from the fog, with eyes as bright as lighthouse beacons and blazing orange like a forest fire. It was spindly and black with quick, long movements and limbs that stretched impossible distances as it walked over the tops of the tombstones.

It stopped at Elliot's grave, hopping over the chasmal hole, and then sprinted over the gardens, vanishing beneath his window.

Elliot leaned forward until his nose pressed against the window frame, his slow, forceful breaths – aided heavily by the air tank tubes strung across his face – clouded the glass. For another few agonizing, silent minutes – he saw nothing. The only sound was the hissing of his air tank, and his own fingertips sliding anxiously down the surface of the glass.

A heavy thud shook him free from his trance. He gasped, his heart fluttering as it skipped a beat. Elliot craned his head to try and look over his shoulder, but his eyes refused to adjust to the darkness. Meanwhile, he heard someone swearing.

"Bloody hell." The person behind him shredded the expletive through their teeth.

"Hello?" Elliot turned his wheelchair around to face the room. In the dim candlelight, he could make out the limber frame of what appeared to be a young man struggling to regain his balance.

"Yes. I'm … doing really great," the young man growled. "Things are going so well. You really shouldn't leave out your furniture in the middle of your room, you know. Someone could trip." The object of his ire, a firmly upholstered ottoman, received a vengeful kick, followed by a hiss of pain.

"I'm sorry," Elliot said, at a loss for words.

"I doubt that. But it doesn't matter. Should I try that again, or are we satisfied by my entirely graceless entrance?"

"I…"

"Good." The young man plopped down onto the ottoman, sweeping inky black curls away from his face. "I'm sorry, you know, I just wasn't expecting to be hurled into a job like this. It's my first one, and when you called they just sort of threw me in your direction…"

"I am Elliot Dosett," Elliot said haughtily, trying to regain control of the conversation. The young man peered at him over manicured fingertips, adjusting round, silver-rimmed spectacles indignantly.

"Right," he said. "They gave me a name. I guess they didn't think I was smart enough to come up with one on my own." He plunged his hands into his pockets, pulling out an assortment of folded papers, crinkled and stained, as well as an assortment of other objects including a pen, a rubber band, and a lint covered hard candy in the shape of a flower.

"You are the demon I summoned?" Elliot glanced over his shoulder out the window once more, as if there had been some sort of mistake. "I thought you would be less…"

"Awkward?"

"Disappointing."

"Same thing, I suppose. Aha." The young man unfolded a limp piece of paper and shook it out. "James. It's James – Highmore?" he squinted at the paper. "I guess that's right. It sounds like the sort of thing they would conjure up." He chuckled at his own joke.

Elliot found his lack of originality to be considerably less amusing. "There must be some sort of procedure." He was trying desperately to move the conversation forward. "I've never done this before…"

"Neither have I. Thankfully, I have a manual." James lifted a small pocket-sized book as thin as a napkin and open it to a dog-eared page, folding its cover back. "We have to go over the terms of the contract." He slid his glasses down to the end of his nose. "You seem a classic sort of fellow, so I assume you will be paying with your soul." He glanced over the silver rims to affirm this was correct.

Elliot nodded, coughing into his hand. Flecks of bright red blood splattered across his pale skin and he fought to take in another deep breath from his respirator. James set the manual down in his lap and frowned.

"My," the demon said gently, "you are in a bad way."

"The doctors have informed me that I will die in less than a year," Elliot said bitterly, wiping his mouth with the back of his hand.

"Surely, you don't intend to?" James stood and walked over to inspect him, curious. "That would not give us very much time. Well, I'm not sure what you want accomplished quite yet, but I can only assume..."

"I intend to live well into my old age," Elliot said. "In the end you will have my soul, but it is just as well. I am not destined for heaven anyway."

"Now," James set a hand on the young man's shoulder, "that's no way to think."

Elliot looked down at the demon's hand and furrowed his brow. "Do not presume to touch me."

James recoiled as if he had been bitten. "Sorry."

"What do I have to sign in?" Elliot asked, tacking on dryly, "Blood?"

"If you'd like," James said helpfully, reaching into his finely-tailored coat to withdraw a slim, folded piece of paper. "Although ink is sufficient. They just need a print of your blood somewhere. Or some other bodily fluid, but blood *is* traditional." He rubbed the crisp paper between his fingers, mulling over a thought. "You know," he said finally. "People don't just summon demons – pardon me – for the hell of it. They usually want something, badly. And it's more than just being afraid to die, isn't it? So what do you want? Your father's company?" He held Elliot's gaze as he spoke, sounding every bit lost and confused as he stumbled to find familiar ground.

"It is more than that," Elliot said, and he looked away, reaching up to brush a thick lock of straight black hair away from his eyes. The candlelight glinted off threads of premature grey. "They treat me like nothing."

"Who does?" James prompted.

"Father. His wife...my elder half-brother, Clarence." He sighed. "I want their respect. And I want them all dead." He narrowed his eyes. "My father is tired of paying my bills. I am an expense, and I bring in nothing to make it worth his while. He is going to send me to a hospital where, if I'm lucky, he will pay for my care. If not... who knows? One hears things, horrible things about patients abandoned by their families. I don't want him to have the power to hurt me like that. I don't want anyone to have power over me ever again."

"I can't imagine..." James was momentarily put off by this sudden outburst of sincerity. "But it ... still seems rather vague, doesn't it?"

Elliot ground his teeth, blood tinged spittle bubbling between them. "He didn't want me. He only allowed me to live here to keep the family name out of the workhouses. Now he won't even try to keep me from going mad in a room no larger than a cell, chained to a bed and drugged out of mind... I could make so many *improvements* to his company, but he will hear none of it.

He only wants Clarence, that stupid braggart who never did anything useful…!" He was getting too worked up. He had to slow down, taking another deep breath.

James stared at him with owlish, unblinking blue eyes.

"Let me sign the contract," Elliot said when he had recovered himself.

"…Of course." James flicked his wrist, flipping open the folded paper. "We can iron out any thorny details later."

Hell was a fire hazard. And certainly not up to code.

Lady flipped through a thick stack of papers, shoving another side with his elbow and sending yet another careening off the edge of his desk. He wondered how many contractors had to die before he qualified for an office renovation, and if relocation would get him out of notarizing demon contracts for a day. It was a prestigious position, they had told him. It was leagues above Soul Processing and it meant he would have his own workspace. They did not tell him that Contract Auditor was shorthand for "shoving around a lot of paper and spilling a lot of ink".

To add insult to injury, they had tossed him into the demon department, because the angelic one had already filled up. His only consolation to being the most miserable auditor in existence was that he got to send people howling into the black pits of eternity and assign demons to rip apart their souls.

That part was a little fun.

He heard the door open, and then he heard it hit a pile of books. He smirked and opened up a drawer, shoving a few crinkled papers inside and slamming it shut again.

"Did you know you have a tower of books just looming right next to your door?" an annoyed voice asked, a wiry body weaving its way through the columns of paper.

"It was intended to be a barricade," Lady said, adjusting thick black-framed glasses. "I see it has failed."

"Keeping me out, or keeping yourself in?" His intern brought two white cups of coffee down to rest on the desk, the sides brown from so much having spilled. That had possibly been caused by the doorway.

"Well I can't very well leave myself with an escape route when I set fire to the joint, now can I?" Lady scowled at him, hands roaming his desk for the packets of sugar he knew he kept. "That ruins the whole damn point."

"I guess. Oh, this came for you." His intern produced a slip of paper, with the harsh, square sort of lettering that only came from the hands of corporate.

Lady plucked it from his fingers and flipped it open, brown sugar eyes scanning it from top to bottom as he sipped his coffee.

"Another audit. Wonderful. I can't believe it." Lady sighed and flung the paper down onto the desk, watching it skid and stir up dust. "Henry is such a waste of sulphur." He pursed his lips pettishly and sipped his coffee again.

"You know that disgusting bastard sent another contract to my desk signed in vaginal fluids?"

"Is that why he's being audited?" The intern tilted his head.

"No. It's because he and some other bastard from the seventh ring have filed a claim for the same soul. And if I don't go sort it out, I'm going to be hearing it from the higher ups now until well, the next time a demon cocks something up." The auditor rubbed his face, groaning into his moleskin gloves. "Why aren't you any help, Frank?"

"Well, to be direct, sir, there isn't much I can do," the intern replied, wincing at the much-hated diminutive of his actual name – Francis. "I fetch your coffee, you throw papers around. We eat our lunch, I clean something and then we go home."

"You've cleaned something?" Lady asked dryly, looking around the ash heap of an office. "You're fired. Now, be a dear and hand me that bag, will you?"

Francis looked around for the item that Lady's wiggling fingers indicated. His eyes settled on a shiny leather briefcase that, when lifted, weighed little less than a small house.

"I don't think I should be left alone," Francis said, thinking the same of his boss.

"Don't fret. You will be fine. Just remember everything I have taught you."

"Let the answering machine pick up everything and don't speak to Jerome from accounting."

"Good man. And our emergency procedure?"

"There is whiskey in the bottom cabinet of the bookcase."

"See? You will do just fine." Lady furrowed his brow, popping up the brass clamps of the leather briefcase. The top sprang open and he gathered up the mess of papers inside, dropping them gracelessly to the floor before replacing them with a neater, clipped stack.

"When will you be back?" Francis was already experiencing a strange sense of abandonment, the same as any child overly attached to a parent.

"Hard to say. Tomorrow, or a thousand years from now. But that is how these things go." Lady glanced distractedly around his office, as if to make sure he wasn't forgetting anything. "Well, off I go then, I suppose." He shut the briefcase and snapped the clips back into place. "Send a message to the higher ups and let them know I'm on my way... if they know I'm gone maybe they won't bother you so much." He picked up his briefcase and sighed as he walked over to the fireplace, stepping carefully over a slovenly pile of ashes and ducking underneath its low lip.

The fireplace belched a cloud of acrid black smoke. Francis wheezed and looked away, his eyes flooding with irritated tears. He wiped them away, coughing again as he stepped close to bend and look up the chimney... but his boss was gone.

CHAPTER 2

Metal rings screeched as they slid over their rod, and thick blue curtains pulled back – allowing obscene shafts of afternoon sunlight to penetrate the heavy gloom of the bedchamber.

"Good morning, my lord," James said cheerfully as Elliot's face scrunched up as tightly as it could against the unwelcome flood of light.

"Fucking hell." The young lord threw his hands up to cover his eyes.

"Don't touch your face like that, my lord. You are going to give yourself blemishes."

Elliot lowered his hands carefully and glowered at the man who was strutting around his room, humming as he prepared a morning ritual.

"What time is it?" Elliot demanded.

"It is nearly tea time, sir," James said, grasping the handles of Elliot's wheelchair and pushing it closer to the bed. For the first time, Elliot was able to get a good look at the demon. The creature who had been summoned from the pits of hell was actually quite tall and gangly, with a mess of black curls and a plump, almost boyish red mouth. His skin was ashen, his eyes – rimmed with thick black lashes – were cerulean. Over a solemn, carefully tailored grey suit he wore a loose white coat – the kind a doctor might wear – and his round, silver-rimmed glasses settled carefully on the end of a pert, sharp nose as he bent to lower the slats for Elliot's feet on the wheelchair.

He did not look anything like a demon. Although he faintly resemble the family accountant.

"Is it that late?" James' words finally caught up to him, and Elliot pressed his palms into the bed, pushing himself farther up. "How could you let me sleep so long?"

"You were tired. You had a long night. I gave you morphine," James said innocently, "for your pain."

"Morphine…?" No wonder his head felt so thick.

"I am your doctor, after all," James said, smiling brightly as he pulled back the covers, intending to help Elliot out of bed.

A firm palm against his chest stopped any progress from being made.

"I would like something to eat first," Elliot said curtly.

"Your father has invited you for tea," James informed him pleasantly, stuffing his hands underneath Elliot's thighs and lifting him slightly, pulling him around until his legs were resting over the side of the bed. Elliot settled his hands on the demon's shoulders, brow furrowing.

"What does my father want with me?" He felt his stomach twist into a familiar knot, fearing the worst.

"I don't know," James said. "But I am more than certain he will tell you." He walked over towards Elliot's wardrobe and pulled open the doors, reaching inside for a grey and burgundy outfit already prepared.

"What made you decide to be my doctor?" Elliot asked, his eyes following the demon's every movement.

"It seemed to make the most sense. You need me to stay close to you, and your last nurse was tragically let go."

"Let go?"

"Let go off the balcony, I mean." James smirked. "Don't worry, I swept her up this morning."

"...Fantastic." Elliot sighed. "And I suppose you know everything there is about my sort of care?"

"Not quite," James said, plucked up the shoulders of Elliot's nightshirt and pulling it over his head, slipping a stiff white dress shirt down in its place. "But I found another manual."

Elliot rolled his eyes. "Of course."

"It says that if you display difficult or aggressive behavior, I am encouraged to medicate you into a stupor." James slid striped grey trousers over long, pale legs.

"Don't you dare," Elliot snipped.

"That sounded a little aggressive, my lord..." James' suggestion was interrupted by a sound smack across the face.

"Ow," James looked up, knitting his brows together. "That was a joke."

"I don't care for your jokes," Elliot said hotly.

"My, you are ill-tempered," James muttered, pulling the burgundy silk vest over Elliot's arms, quick fingers sliding the buttons through their loops. "I read somewhere that it does not become a gentleman to be so badly natured. Maybe there is a reason your father doesn't like you."

A long silence followed this statement as Elliot tilted his head back just enough for James to thread a black silk tie through the starched wings of his collar.

"Do you like me?" Elliot asked curiously.

James knelt and started on thin black socks, followed by polished black shoes. "Not particularly."

"Oh." Elliot went quiet again, and James pulled a brush through his hair.

The grey wool frock coat was the last item presented. Elliot slipped his arms through it, adjusting it primly.

"I don't see why I *should* like you." James said, retrieving a new air tank from the collection of supplies. It gleamed in the light – he had spent a good hour polishing them the night before. "After all, you haven't given me much of a reason." He set the tank down, long enough to slide his arms over Elliot – one around his back and the other underneath his legs, lifting him up and transferring him smoothly form bed to wheelchair. He switched out the old tank and the new, placing it in its custom holster on the back of the wheelchair, arranging the thick tubes so that they did not interfere as much with Elliot's movements. "You act like everything must be so straight-laced – you get what you want, I get your soul – but it's not that way at all. We can be friends. At the very *least* you don't have to look so dour all the time. Demonic contracts aren't what they used to be. Once upon a time we just followed you like withered shadows, whispering in your ear and tempting you to do even worse than you planned and rubbing our palms together like scheming thieves."

"So what happened?" Elliot asked, settling his hand on the arms of his chair.

"Our department received a renovation. New management took over, and marketing decided that the classic tempter approach was 'far too old century'. They streamlined the process, gave us a quota, and told us to smile more."

"You know a good deal for someone who is so new. And bad at his job," Elliot added, just to needle.

"It was all in the training literature." James sounded a little hurt. "Am I doing so poorly? I thought I was doing rather well at getting things accomplished." He started pushing Elliot towards the door, which opened for them on its own.

"It is not as bad as it could be," Elliot said begrudgingly. "I haven't died yet. Although for the sake of my father, you could try acting a little more solemn."

"Hmm." James nodded. "I could try."

Lord Hiram Dosett was trying to enjoy his tea, but that was not going entirely as planned.

For one thing, it was the wrong kind.

He liked to think that he was the type of person who didn't ask for very much. And tea time was one of the single luxuries he had manage to nestle into his otherwise tightly packed schedule. Tranquility was rare for a man of his prominence. Even rarer for the foremost steel tycoon of the era. He suffered through breakfast with his intolerable wife and dilettante eldest son. He endured morning meetings with tiresome investors. He drudged through mountains of paperwork that never seemed to end and all he asked was that at precisely four o'clock he be allowed to step away from his desk, sit at a small carved table in front of an expansive bay window overlooking the estate gardens, and revel in the quiet of his study while enjoying a delicate cup of steaming hot tea and crisp triangular pastries.

Of course, today of all days, things were simply refusing to go his way. One of his meetings ran late, putting him behind schedule by nearly a quarter of an hour. When he had finally been able to settle down for his much desired respite, he had been expecting rich Assam tea and chocolate-filled pastries.

Instead, he was presented with a far weaker Hyson brew, and currant teacakes.

Hiram absolutely despised currants.

Elliot happened to love them.

"Good afternoon, father." Elliot's quiet, yet resonant voice drifted across the room.

Hiram clenched the fragile handle of his teacup.

"Good afternoon, Elliot." He did not look up as his son's wheelchair made its way soundlessly across the floor, impelled by a tall, awkward man too thin to fill out the long white doctor's coat he was wearing. Not only that, but he appeared far too young to be a man with any *reputable* practice. "Who is this?"

"My new doctor," Elliot said, as he was settled across the table. "He was sent from the Mother's Mercy hospital this morning. My other nurse was ... called home."

The doctor smiled secretively.

Hiram scrutinized the young man mercilessly as he stepped lightly around Elliot's wheelchair and began to pour his tea. "Do you have a name?" the lord asked.

"James Highmore, my lord," the young doctor said, bowing his head and tipping the teapot over Elliot's cup, filling it almost to the brim.

"I do not take it with cream," Elliot said, his fingers twitching in agitation.

James nodded and smiled, and then picked up the small creamer, filling the teacup the rest of the way out of spite.

Elliot's lips thinned, but he didn't say a word. James set the teacup on its saucer and presented it to his charge, all smiles and good grace.

Hiram watched the curious exchange but did not remark on it, choosing instead to prod at his slice of currant cake with a small dessert fork.

"You are wondering why I bothered to have you brought here," Hiram said, addressing his younger son.

"Yes," Elliot said, turning supplicant, inquiring grey eyes to his father. "I have seen you at supper, but you never mentioned something might be pressing..." He found it hard to swallow, struggling not to wrestle for each breath his air tank supplied. It was always like this. He would get worked up and anxious, and if things got worse, he would pass out. He suspected that was the reason his father always lost patience with him during their conversations, but he could not help it. Every time Hiram summoned him for a private audience, Elliot was waiting to hear the dark words that would send him towards the fate he dreaded most. He waited for the words *'hospital'*, *'scrupulous care'*, and *'cost efficient'*.

He feared them so much, that even the presence of a demon was not enough to comfort him.

James was quiet, standing dutifully behind Elliot's chair. He watched Hiram closely, as if the lord's face was an open resource for every piece of information he needed to know.

"Do you remember your aunt, Lady Violet Clifton?" Hiram asked, placing his fingertips together.

Elliot blinked, thrown off by the unexpected direction of the conversation.

"Ah..." He paused, sipping his tea and making a face at its unpleasantly weak, milky taste. "Vaguely."

"You were young when you last met. She has heard about your *condition*, and she wishes to pay her respects."

"Respects?" Elliot asked dryly. "I am not dead yet."

"Soon enough," Hiram said, his voice edged with steel.

Elliot set his cup down with a loud clatter, coughing into his hand. James produced a clean white handkerchief for him from his sleeve.

"You will receive her properly. She will be here within days and I will not have you dragging yourself out of bed midday, insulting her with your foul mood and polluting the atmosphere of this house." Hiram was disgusted. "She will arrive with knowledge of your condition, but you need not snivel for her pity. Act like someone I would claim, or I swear I will lock you in the attic until you expire and I have to send the servants up to investigate the smell."

Elliot cringed, coughing again and crumpling up the handkerchief in his fist. "Yes, Father. As you command." He paused, unable to resist adding sardonically, "Shall I stand up and walk for her as well?"

"If you can manage." Hiram turned his glare towards James. "You will see that he is his best when she arrives, or else make up some excuse as to why he cannot be seen that day."

James nodded. "Of course." He set his hand on Elliot's shoulder. "He will be in pristine condition."

"I am glad to hear it." Hiram glanced over at his son's untouched plate. "Are you finished?"

Elliot nodded. He did not have the stomach even for currant teacakes.

"You may go, then." Hiram settled back in his chair. "There is nothing more we need discuss. And," he turned his attention once more to James, "if he gives you trouble, give him morphine. You should have plenty, I ordered an entire case." He settled his gaze on Elliot, giving him a long, pointed look. "Enough to kill a horse, I would not wonder."

Elliot drew himself up straight in his chair, giving him father a cold smile before James pulled him back and, with a bow, turned him around and started out the door.

"I don't like him at all," James whispered, once they were a safe distance from the study.

"You are not the first," Elliot said through his teeth.

There was a pause, and then James added, "I do not think I will be giving you very much morphine."

The Dosett estate was much like Lady Clifton remembered it: somber and austere. Everything from the manicured lawn to the precisely trimmed hedges was done with symmetry in mind. It all reflected its master rather well... strict, with the personality of a grape.

"Bloody hell, where have we landed?" Henry peeled back the curtain from the carriage window, peering out warily. "It is grim, I will give you that. Do you think it's haunted?"

"Would that matter to you, if it was?" Violet asked, quirking an eyebrow at him.

He shrugged. "Well, if I have to keep my eyes peeled for anyone I know..."

She shook her head. "We are here to meet Elliot. You are getting off easily with this encounter... my sister only met William a handful of times, and none of them left much of an impression."

"What about her husband?"

"Hiram never met William."

"This will be no fun, then, is what you are saying." Henry squirmed in his seat, shifting anxiously like a child with too much energy for long distance carriage rides. "I hate this. When are we going to step out?"

"Never," Lady Clifton said distractedly, her eyes drifting again towards the window. "I am never going to let you out."

"That isn't funny."

The carriage rolled to a stop at last. Henry did not wait for the footman to open the door. He grasped the handle and sprang out, sighing in relief when his heels hit gravel. He straightened his stiff jacket, rolling his shoulders and neck as he looked around, surveying the estate from a new angle.

"Violet!" A dainty woman, very short and very blonde, emerged from the house. "How good to see you again!"

Lady Clifton emerged gracefully from the carriage, aided by a footman, and forced a smile.

"Lucy," she said, "it has been far too many years."

The shorter woman – Lucy – ran up to Violet and they threw their arms around each other. Henry had just enough time to evaluate this newcomer and decide that he wasn't going to like her.

"William," Lucy pulled away from Violet just long enough to turn to the man she perceived as her sister's husband. "It is good to see you again, as well."

Henry flashed her his most winning smile, thinking belatedly that the lord he was impersonating might not have done so. "Oh, sure, far too long." He swept up her hand in his and brought it up to his lips for a kiss. She flushed, and Lady Violet rolled her eyes.

"You are certainly in good spirits," Lucy said. "When last we heard you were horribly ill. I am so pleased to see you have made a full and swift recovery."

"Not so pleased as I," Henry said, already enjoying himself far too much. "And, you know," he lowered his voice conspiratorially, "I daresay that it was the hand of

God himself, brought to me in a vision, that wrenched me free from the jaws of death."

Lucy's light green eyes widened. "No," she said, pressing her hand to her breast. "You must tell me more."

"*Well,*" Henry pulled her arm through his, starting to walk back towards the estate. "It was the strangest thing. As I was tossing and turning on my death bed, certain that any moment I would open my eyes to see the grim reaper standing before me, ready to claim my soul… it happened."

"What happened?" Lucy clutched his arm.

"A tall, handsome man – no, a golden-haired angel – appeared before me wreathed in light."

Violet slid a gloved hand over her face.

"And he did not say a word, but he reached into my chest and cupped his hands around my heart, and all of the breath was stolen from my body. But when he released me, I was rejuvenated. Whole and alive once more… I swear to you, madame, in that moment, I was a new man – entirely different than the one who had gone to bed."

"That is brilliant!" Lucy declared, glancing over her shoulder. "Violet, did he tell you of this?"

"I was there," Violet said tersely.

"And you witnessed this celestial being also?"

"She had to look away," Henry beamed. "She could not behold the sight of his glory."

Violet gave him the darkest glare she could manage.

"It is simply amazing," Lucy sighed. "I have always thought, you know, that the dying could see God. It is so splendid and *rare* to have confirmation! But of course," she smiled shyly up at Henry. "I am glad to have you returned to us."

"Madame, I find it only right to assume that God's very intention in restoring me was such that I could hasten here to relay my story to you." Henry pulled away from her, giving her hand a final lingering kiss. "How fortunate I am that he has allowed me to recall it so vividly, all the better to disclose every detail to you."

Lucy's cheeks flushed again, and she turned to Violet, her lips pursed. "For shame, Violet! I was not prepared to receive William in such good spirits. How dare you give me no warning!"

Violet could only offer a helpless shrug.

"Well," Lucy chattered on, "you two have had a long journey, and I am sure you would like to rest. The butler will show you to your rooms…"

"I would like," Lady Violet interjected, "to see Elliot as soon as possible. If I may."

Lucy frowned, an expression which Henry thought far better suited her face.

"If you would like, I will have him sent for," she said. "But really, there is no hurry… he will be present at supper."

"Indeed, my dear, there is no hurry." Henry took Violet by the hand, squeezing her fingers. "Let us retire together to freshen up. If he keels over at the supper table, we do not wish his last sight to be his disheveled aunt in her mussed traveling dress."

Violet closed her eyes, as if she were straining every nerve not to punch him in the face.

When she opened them again, she smiled.

"Of course," she said, squeezing his fingers in return. "You are quite correct." She turned back to Lucy. "We would be grateful for a chance to refresh ourselves."

Lucy smiled again and nodded, waving a maid forward. "It is such a treat for us to have you here, I honestly cannot emphasize how ecstatic I am, truly."

Henry grinned. "Truthfully, madam, we are just as elated."

The dining room rug was very disagreeable. Henry could not bring himself to get over it. And whoever decided that dark wood paneling on walls was a good idea should have been dragged out into the streets and shot.

He was going to have to try very hard not to be too distracted by it at supper.

Lady Lucy Dosett was already seated when they arrived. She rose to show off her son, Clarence, who was head and shoulders taller than she and similarly golden-haired. Henry dismissed him at a glance and sat down almost immediately, picking up his silverware and fiddling with it distractedly, his eyes darting around the room and drinking in every poorly made choice. A hand came down on the back of his, slamming his palm and the fork he was holding to the table. He shot a glare over at Violet, but obediently replaced his fork.

Lucy was carrying on about Clarence and is accomplishments. Henry was only half-listening, as Lucy was not the sort of woman who needed a response to continue the conversation. He managed to glean that she had other younger children somewhere, but they had already eaten. He presumed that they were now stashed in a closet, bound and gagged, only to be unleashed whenever it was attractive for Lady Dosett to have them around. That, he thought, was the only proper way to store children.

Lord Hiram entered the room next, and Henry could not help but think he looked constipated. The lord of the house kissed his sister-in-law and shook Henry's hand, his grip firm – the sort of grasp accustomed to closing deals. He took his seat at the head of the table, and bowed his head. The others also lowered their chins and closed their eyes. Henry looked around, confused.

"Amen." Lord Hiram looked up, and Henry's eyebrows shot towards his hairline. Of course. Grace. That was a custom.

He pinched the stem of his wine glass between his fingers and lifted it cordially, smiling.

"Cheers." He drained the dry Carménère.

There was a slight pause. Lord Hiram lifted his eyebrow and parted his lips, as if his intention was to comment, but he was interrupted by the sound of large wheels rolling over wooden floors.

A young man, no older than eighteen, made his entrance into the dining room. He was seated in an expensive wheelchair, propelled by a tall doctor who appeared only a few years older. Henry's eyes narrowed and he swallowed a cough as he caught wind of an unpleasant odor, and he was sure he was the only one that noticed.

This 'doctor' stank of sulphur. All young demons did.

"Things just became *far* more interesting," Henry whispered to Violet, letting the statement hang cryptically; knowing it would needle her that he did so.

"Elliot," Lady Violet said, donning her most sincere smile. "It is so good to see you again."

"Aunt Violet," Elliot bowed his head, and his air tank hissed. Henry's fingers twitched. That sound was going to end up getting on his nerves.

"I am sorry I'm late," Elliot said apologetically. "There was a mishap."

"Well, it seems you have recovered from it." Hiram gestured curtly. "Come to the table."

The demon doctor pushed Elliot closer to the table, his head turning to look at Henry. Cerulean eyes scanned him up and down, and then the demon smiled, flashing white incisors – tinged slightly pink.

Henry wondered what sort of 'mishap' they had run into.

Supper was served without much ceremony, as Lord Hiram did not seem to be the kind to indulge in unnecessary pomp. They began with a savory soup, which Henry did not much relish, and would have welcomed any sort of distraction that did not come in the form of Lady Lucy's incessant blathering.

Unfortunately, she was dominating the table with talk of a hunting trip she was organizing for later that year, and Henry wondered if demons could die of boredom.

Before he could find out, he decided to redirect the conversation.

"So, Elliot." He leaned forward, cutting off Lucy in the middle of her sentence. "I hear you are dying. How is that going?"

Silence.

You could have heard a pin drop.

Elliot raked his fork across an empty space on his plate. It made an awful screeching sound that made everyone's teeth ache.

"Well, I am still alive," Elliot said. "So presumably...not very well."

Henry laughed while the demon doctor smiled, clearing Elliot's plate away demurely.

"We do not like to discuss it," Hiram said, firmly taking hold of the conversation by its reins. "It is a dour subject."

"Oh, for sure." Henry waved his hand airily. "Death is a deplorable subject. But we were speaking of hunting, and I was reminded."

"They have given me less than a year," Elliot said, not about to turn down the attention for his father's benefit, and all too pleased to be seditious. "Although the infection could overtake my lungs and kill me any day between now and Christmas."

"And *Clarence*," Lady Lucy interjected, trying desperately to distract, "has absolutely *excelled* in his tennis competitions this year..."

"*William* is quite fond of tennis," Lady Violet responded, her eyes boring into the demon's skull. "I'm sure he would love to engage Clarence in a match during our stay."

"Well," Clarence replied in the tone of someone who thought they were witty, "I can't say that I will let you win ... but I promise to hold back for the first few rounds!"

Henry's smile was reminiscent of a shark. "I always win."

Another lull formed in the conversation as the remainders of the game course were swept away and replaced by crystal dishes of lemon ice.

Elliot's face reddened and he made an odd sound, obviously trying to suppress a cough. He spooned some of the citrus ice into his mouth to suck on, hoping that would help.

The demon doctor set a hand on his lord's shoulder and looked to Hiram.

"The master is quite exhausted, I think, from all of the evening's excitement," he said soothingly. "I should like to give him some medicine and put him to bed."

Elliot looked annoyed and like he might protest, but the demon's knuckles whitened as they gripped his shoulder and the young man remained silent. Henry was intrigued.

"Fine, fine," Hiram said. "Send him off, then."

"Thank you for having me," Elliot said, his voice a touch raspy. "Goodnight, Father. And-" He nodded to Violet. "Aunt Violet."

The demon doctor pulled back the wheelchair and then started for the exit. Henry's eyes followed them the entire way. Only when they vanished did he steal a glance at Violet, who was also watching them closely, but not for the same reasons.

Henry spooned some lemon ice into his mouth, cringing inwardly as Lady Lucy started her chatter up once more. Something about a garden party.

He found himself wondering if, while Violet was getting what she wanted from Elliot, he might have a word with his demon.

CHAPTER 3

His coughing was always worse at night, as if his body was trying so hard to stay alive that it did not want to succumb even to sleep. He had convinced James to give him morphine, even if the demon was now reluctant to do so. Yet his coughing still woke him up in the middle of the night, enough so that when his fit finally settled, he was still awake to see the door open, and a single burning lamp slice through the darkness.

He heard the bedroom door shut, and he squinted.

"James?" he asked, as the lamp hovered closer. He could not make out any distinct features until it had settled right beside his bed and the soft, heart-shaped face of Violet Clifton leaned over, close to his face.

"Hello, Elliot," she whispered, setting the lamp down on a small bedside table.

"Aunt Violet?" He struggled to sit up, but that wasn't happening. His arms were too weak from the medication. He fell back to his pillows helplessly, looking up at her in confusion. "It's very late."

"I know, but I had to come see you." She touched the side of his face. "I was worried, when you left supper as you did…"

"I apologize," Elliot said, some of his usual curtness returning as his grogginess was leaving him.

"Do not feel the need to do so." She smiled kindly, resting a hand on his chest lightly – careful of the thick tubes. "But you *are* the entire reason for my visit."

He didn't bother to ask why, although the curiosity was eating him alive. Violet Clifton had seen him a grand total of twice during his childhood, and had never so much as written during all of the years in between. Why she had come all of this way to see him, so close to the end of his life, was anybody's guess.

"You know…" She slipped her hand further down. "I always regretted not getting to know you better. But with William, he is always so busy. And with him having been ill for so long, it has been difficult to even leave the house." She sighed, and her hand slipped under the thick bedcover. "That is what compelled me to come see you. I know William needed someone by his side, and I wanted to make certain you had someone by yours. And he has made such a miraculous recovery. Who knows?" She winked. "Maybe I am good luck."

Her hand found its way underneath his nightshirt, between his burning thighs. He hissed at the contact but could not do much to pull away, even lifting his hand to try and grab hers felt like it was taking an eternity.

"Stop," he said sharply. "What do you think you are doing?"

"Someone told me," she said quietly, "that you are not dead from the waist down, only weak."

"My legs can't hold me up," he said. "That is all. And have you tried walking around with an air tank?"

She slid her hands over his scrotum, trailing a delicately pointed nail to the base of his cock before taking it in her hands. He was still soft enough that she could take the entire thing in her palm. She began to stroke the supple folds of his skin, feeling him start to harden as she slid her thumb over the head, feeing a streak of glistening wetness.

He was not circumcised. How very un-Christian.

He groaned, his eyes rolling back, and he hardened completely. He turned his head away from her, his fingers knotting in the sheets as she made faster, even strokes up and down his shaft, her fingers spread so that she touched base and head at all times with each movement. Her other hand pulled the covers down, and she looked up at him briefly before lowering her head, her hot pink tongue flickering over the salty skin of his thighs, the dips of his jutting hip bones. She opened her mouth as wide as she could, and took his scrotum into her mouth, sucking on it loudly, her hand moving as quickly over his cock as it could go.

Elliot moaned deeply and turned his head as far as he could into his pillow, his body jerking with the orgasm, and his seed poured from the tip of his cock, dripping down the sides and spilling onto her fingers.

She gathered up as much of it as she could on her fingertips, her other hand pulling the covers back up to his waist. He looked at her, struggling to breathe properly, unsure of how angry he should be. Lady Clifton only smiled at him serenely, and stood, her covered hand still cupped as she picked up her lamp with the other.

"Thank you, Elliot," she said, and leaned over to kiss his forehead, sticky with sweat. She then turned to leave, her skirts rustling mutedly as she crossed the room and he saw the light disappear.

Once she was standing in the hallway, Violet set her lamp down on the floor, reaching into her bodice to withdraw a tightly folded square of paper. She shook her hand so that it fell open, and she smeared Elliot's thick white will across the bottom of the paper, right underneath his name.

"A piece of him," she said quietly. She lifted her thumb to rest against her mouth, pausing only briefly before biting down on the corner, hissing with pain as a bead of dark blood welled up. She waited until she could taste it, bitter like iron, and then smeared the side of her thumb over the next unoccupied space of the paper, next to her own name.

"A piece of me," she said, and folded the paper again.

As soon as she drew her pinched fingers over the last smart crease, the white paper faded to grey, and then the entire contract crumbled to ash in her hands.

She sucked in a deep breath. It was done now, there was no turning back.

At least Henry would get a fine meal from Elliot's bitter, bitter soul.

"Your name is James, is it?"

James nearly dropped the box of needles he was holding. He adjusted his glasses and spun around, eyes scanning the room until he spotted the intruder, leaning against the low mantle of the anteroom fireplace and fiddling with the decorative china figures.

It was that demon he had seen at the dining room table. James groaned inwardly, returning the box to its place in his large black doctor's bag.

"Neat cover-up, a doctor," the elder demon prompted helpfully. "I never would have thought of it, personally. But it's also a bit too … nerdy for me, I guess. You have to know stuff, don't you? About the body and medicine and the like. That never really was my area."

"I'm sorry," James said, losing his patience and his nerve at the same time. "Did you want something from me?"

"I didn't know there was already a demon in this estate," the older demon said smoothly. "Are you under a contract?"

"I was summoned by Elliot Dosett," James said, drawing out the statement deliberately, keeping his gaze with the elder demon level. Something on the other's face shifted subtly, his smile withering a little.

"Well, that is very interesting." The elder stroked his chin. "The kid in a wheelchair? How droll."

"I don't see what is so farcical about it," James murmured.

"I am Henry, by the way."

"I didn't ask."

The fireplace rumbled. Henry snatched his hand away, taking several steps back and looking like a startled cat. James clutched his medicine bag as the mouth of the fireplace disgorged a rolling nebulosity of thick black smoke and flecks of grey ash.

The entire room smelled like sulphur. James coughed, his eyes watering with irritation. He rubbed at them behind his glasses, and when the smoke finally cleared, he could make out a peculiar looking man standing in the middle of the ornate rug, carrying a leather briefcase and dusting himself off prissily.

"I hope they gave me the right address this time," the man muttered, adjusting dark-framed glasses and shaking out a mess of auburn ringlets. James blinked, and when he opened his eyes again, the man was only a few inches away, waving a gloved hand in the demon's face.

"Hello there!" the man shouted much louder than was necessary. "Can you see me?"

"Yes!" James crinkled his nose and swatted at the annoying hand, the size of a child's.

"Oh, good. Then this must be right." The man seemed satisfied as he stepped back. James had always considered himself short, as far as demons went, being only 5'10". But this man was lucky to scrape six inches over five feet. His smart black shoes had a slight heel.

"Hello," James said, attempting to take the reins of the situation. "You are...?"

The newcomer regarded him snottily. "Meriwether Hayward, CPDCA. But just Lady, if you please."

"Lady...?" James' brow creased.

"It is gender neutral," the newcomer said patiently.

"Not really." Henry smirked.

"Well, go with it anyway." Lady waved his hand, setting his briefcase down on a nearby coffee table and popping it open. "Hello, Henry, you vulgar piece of shit."

"What sort of trouble am I in, now? You are never good news for me." Henry stepped closer, and briefly regarded James with sparkling eyes.

Lady reached into his briefcase and withdrew a stack of papers held together with a shiny clip.

"Wait," James held up a hand, still a few frames behind in the conversation. "What is a CP... whatever those letters were after your name?"

"C-P-D-C-A. Certified Public Demon Contract Auditor. Are you James Highmore?"

"Yes..."

Lady tugged one of the papers free of the clip, smacking it flat against James' chest. "Congratulations, an audit on your first job."

"An *audit?*" Henry tore his paper from Lady's hands, turning it over in disbelief. "You have got to be kidding me. Who issued this?"

"Talk to your supervisors. I am just doing my job," Lady said. "From what I understand both of you signed contracts laying claim to the same soul. That is what we call a 'no-no' in my department."

"The same soul? I don't understand." James brought his paper closer to his face, scrutinizing every word. "Elliot performed the summoning ritual and I was the only demon who answered. Who else could possibly...?"

"Oh come on, Lady. Surely you can let this slide," Henry said, throwing his arm around the smaller man's slender shoulders. "Just move a few names around, it doesn't have to be a big deal. We both know you like me far too much to see me chained to the floor of Hell for a thousand years for something so miniscule."

Lady scoffed. "Do I, really?"

Henry sucked on his teeth, sliding his arm away. "You are a cold bitch, you know. One would think you were straight from the ninth circle."

"I'm not going to enjoy this anymore than either of you. I can think of a dozen more interesting things to do than follow you around and take notes. But that is how this is going to be, until the contract is up and I see which one of you is the unscrupulous bastard that I get to bring down." Lady flitted a glance towards Henry. "And I have a feeling I know who *that* will be."

"I don't understand the logistics," James said, still confused as to how this could have happened. "So we both laid claim to the same soul – big deal! Shouldn't that be between the two of us? Why not let us duke it out? Why does Hell have to get involved?"

"All right." Lady clasped his gloved hands together. "Let's just take this through in stages. So, what do we know about souls?"

James thought about it for a minute, reverting back to his training. "Each is created with the potential to be good and the potential to be evil."

"Broadly." Lady nodded. "And what do we know about Hell?"

"Everyone has a quota," Henry responded. He knew that one far too well.

"Right. And so does Heaven. Along with bonuses and paid vacations, but we are not going to talk about that," Lady groused. "Since every demon has a quota, say – all right, sixty-five souls a year. That is sixty-five *entire* souls that must be documented and accounted for *before* being devoured. Now, what happens if you both lay claim to the same soul?"

"Err..." James looked to Henry for help.

"You have to go halfsies, right?" Lady prompted. "Well, how are you going to document *half* a soul?"

"Uh..."

"You can't. You will document the entire thing. One successful soul-devouring. So *both* of you have filed the paperwork for an entire soul, which means there should be *two*, but only *one* has been devoured. In essence," Lady took a breath. "You have both filled a slot in your quotas while only doing *half* the work."

"All right," Henry nodded. "So far, I don't see a downside."

Lady snorted. "For you, maybe. But what ends up being a small break for you is a kink in the machinery of Hell itself. And you would not believe how one error in accounting can amass to the entire operation breaking down. And do you know what happens when Hell goes out of commission for even an hour?"

"Heaven meets its quota, I imagine," Henry said.

"Pandemonium breaks loose. The damned don't have anywhere to go, so they run around fucking things up even further until we can send grim reapers to collect them all. And then that is hours of labor we have to pay for."

"So the dishonest demon gets chained to the floor of Hell for a thousand years and gets terribly behind on his soul count. That benefits no one, and since when does Hell punish the dishonest? Lady, I see a far brighter future." Henry lifted his hands, as if envisioning it. "I see... an opportunity."

James was already picturing what it would be like to be in manacles for the next thousand years. And none of this was even his fault.

"I know this is a pain in the ass," Henry continued smoothly. "I know that you are tired and run-down from this thankless job. Toiling underneath the severe command of the higher-ups, cowering in the long shadow of Satan – a great corporate authority figure you have never even really *seen*. You are a smudge of ink on His payroll, but your position is ideal! You are so far under His radar that you will never even be suspected."

"Suspected of what? What vile fraud are you suggesting?" Lady folded his arms. "I can't believe I am even entertaining this – Henry Wickes, don't you *dare* try to tempt me...!"

"No, no, my intentions are not so base," Henry cooed, looking hurt as he placed a hand on his chest. "But... think about it, Lady, James and I work so well together..."

James was not sure when this had been established.

"...We can use this situation to our advantage. Violet and Elliot both hold the keys to society's highest circles. They could sign away all sorts of delightful, bitter souls to us, and we could lap them right up. James can have them sign their contracts in blood, and I can have them sign in sexual fluids. You know how fond I am of doing that already."

"Yes." Lady narrowed his eyes. "Your contracts have a tendency to stick to all the others."

"It would never be suspected as being out of the ordinary," Henry's smile broadened. "And it would be practically untraceable, if you keep dismissing any charges that come up. All you have to do is tear up that audit. Send a note back to Hell that there was a mistake – I am sure there is more than one Elliot Dosett in the world, it must happen all of the time. Then we can move on, and do an even greater, more terrible work that is *actually* worthy of Hell. Then James and I fill our quotas – fuck, we can even exceed them – because we will only be doing half the work each time. We will be glutted on souls and you?" He tapped Lady on the shoulder. "I bet you are wondering what you get out of this deal?"

"Besides some time neck-deep in a frozen lake, reflecting my life choices, yes."

"You get all of their pretty eyes," Henry said, pausing for dramatic effect. "Every. Single. One."

Lady licked his lips.

"I know how you love them," Henry hammered on. "Two eyes for every soul, give or take a cripple. Nice, firm eyes that you can break open with your teeth and they pop in your mouth, all jelly-filled and sweet sliding down your throat…"

"All right! All right." Lady held up a hand, pulling a handkerchief from his neatly tailored jacket and dabbing beads of sweat away from his temples. "Don't get…carried away."

"Have I have convinced you?" Henry purred.

"Don't act like it was so difficult," Lady murmured, stuffing his handkerchief back into his jacket pocket. "You're so damn smug that it ought to be fined."

"I don't like this scheme," James protested, knowing his opinion didn't matter but he threw it into the mix anyway. "I don't think it's going to work and it's going to make a lot of people royally *pissed.*"

"You can't think like that, James, you've got to be optimistic," Henry chided. "Disparaging sorts of comments like that are precisely why Lady hasn't received a promotion in almost five hundred years."

Lady was indignant.

"I need both of you to take this seriously," the auditor said, "or we are all going to be speared and roasted over open coals. Is that what you want?"

"It has been a long time," Henry said thoughtfully with a smile, "since I have been speared."

Lady scrunched up his nose. "You are so *vulgar.*"

CHAPTER 4

He dreamt that someone was watching him, though he hesitated to say it was a demon. They sat in the farthest corner of the room, a large, broad frame in a too-small chair. The wood creaked every time they shifted, uncrossing and re-crossing their legs, moonlight glinting off the tops of shiny black shoes. Their face was completely obscured by shadow, but Elliot could hear one hand scratching the other, all too graphic and lurid – clipped nails dragging across poreless skin. The only other thing he could hear was breathing; perfectly in time with the hissing of his air tank.

Everything smelled like clean bandages and powdered drugs. Underneath it all was the faintest scent of rotting meat.

Elliot knew he was sitting up, but for a few horrifying minutes he could not move any part of his body. His arms were limp at his side, too heavy to even drag across the soft white sheets. He tried to turn his head, but it would not budge – he only succeeded in making his neck ache with the strain. Horrified, he briefly considered the possibility of being dead. But why would a dead man be sitting upright, without his pillows stacked behind him to support the weight?

It all loosened up at once. His arms turned to jelly, but he could move them again, and his head lolled as he regained control of his neck. Elliot made a frustrated sound and nearly fell back against his pillows but stopped himself, gasping when he felt nothing was there. His arms flew back and his palms stopped his descent. When he looked back down, he could see he was somehow sitting on the edge of the bed – his legs hanging over the side. He had no memory of how that could have happened.

Tentatively, Elliot pushed himself forward. His nightshirt hiked up and his bare skin brushed over the cool sheets. His feet touched the ground, and he very, very carefully stood up.

Briefly, his knees trembled – and then he was steady. Amazed, Elliot took a cautious step forward. His foot stayed sure, and he was able to follow the first step with another. Elliot lifted his head, encouraged, and focused his attention on the entity in the corner.

A large hand, distinctively male and the color of caramel, extended from the darkness, its fingers curling inwardly towards its palm. It languidly beckoned Elliot forward.

He was moving, getting closer with each step. A voice from the darkness spoke, dark and resonant enough to shake the very foundation of the estate.

"Come closer, boy," it said. "Let us have a good look at you."

He stopped just inches away, but he still could not make out much more than a body, head and neck still blotted out. The watcher wore a suit such that Elliot had never seen before, obviously pressed and well-tailored, but cut in a sort of way where all of the edges of were razor sharp. It was navy with white pinstripes, accentuated by a straight crimson tie.

"Come closer," the voice rumbled again. Elliot was not sure how much closer he could venture without sitting in this person's lap. He took one more hesitant step forward and then that caramel-colored hand snaked out, grabbing him by the wrist and jerking him down until he was nearly doubled-over.

A puff of breath in his face; breath that smelled like cigarettes and black coffee.

"Elliot." The utterance of his name shook him to the core, making his stomach quiver. He looked down and saw the hand that was around his wrist was turning black, and long, curved claws were springing forth from the nail beds – pointed tips digging into his flesh. He hissed and jerked, but the hand tightened, even as blood started dripping down his palm.

"Elliot." This time, it spoke with James' voice.

"James?" Elliot furrowed his brow, his head snapping up. The shadows were split apart by a wide grin full of sharp, metal teeth. The maw opened and emitted a low, thunderous sound like the whirring of gears. The smell of rotting meat grew stronger. Elliot screamed and thrashed, tugging on the hand that held him captive.

"Elliot, Elliot!"

The hand released him. He was falling, and he felt his eyes roll up in the back of his head, darkness swallowing his vision.

"My lord!"

Elliot woke up screaming, with James' hands on his shoulders, pinning them to the mattress. All of his pillows had been dashed to the floor, his sheets were in knots on the other side of the bed. He was shaking, his skin clammy with sweat. His teeth were chattering and he could barely see the demon looming over him, an expression of concern scrawled across his face.

"H-H-Help me." Elliot couldn't breathe, he could barely cough up the words. There was blood in his mouth; it gushed from a vicious tear in his lip that his own teeth had made.

"Henry!" he heard James snarl. "If you would like to help…!"

"Which of these did you say you needed?"

"Laudanum – quick!"

"They all look the same."

Elliot moaned, his entire body seizing. He felt a prick, though his scattered mind was unable to locate the place on his body, and then quickly spreading warmth.

He was able to catch his breath again. He sighed and collapsed onto the bed, a soaking heap.

"You are no goddamn help," he overhead James say.

"I don't know how you doctors get anything done," the other voice replied frankly.

"James?" Elliot knew he sounded like a child calling out for a parent. He hated it, but he felt immediate relief when James' hand closed over his, and an arm slid underneath his back.

"Come on," the demon doctor said gently, "let's get you straightened up." He slid Elliot upwards a few inches towards the headboard, abandoning him only briefly to pick up a number of pillows and arrange them, adjusting Elliot again so he could he could rest comfortably propped up against them. When that was done, he poured a cup of water, holding it up to Elliot's chapped, bleeding lips.

Elliot drank gratefully, taking hold of the cup for himself on the second swallow. He drained about half of the glass before lowering it and looking around the room, his vision slowly returning to normal. Everything looked so bright, but he supposed that was a combination of the morning sunlight and bleariness from the dream.

"James," Elliot grumbled, taking another sip of water. "Close the curtains."

Footsteps, and the curtains slid on their rod. The room was cast in gloom once again.

"My, you're a bit of a vampire, aren't you?" The voice that had replied to James earlier spoke again. "Good morning, Elliot."

The man who spoke was the same one who had accompanied Violet Clifton to dinner. Elliot racked his brain for a name.

"Do you have business with me...?" A name, a name...he studied the man's face before realization hit him.

Shit.

"...Uncle William." Terror buffeted him, knocking a series of anxiety-ridden, chest-tightening coughs right out of his lungs. Elliot briefly recalled the face of Lady Violet Clifton, and the feeling of her hand and mouth as she disappeared between his legs. He could not remember if it had been a dream or not. It had *felt* real, but so did the hand of the mysterious watcher around his wrist.

Maybe that was it. Maybe it had been real, and her husband had found out. Now he would tear Elliot to pieces... and no one would stop him. Hiram would probably send the man a calligraphic 'thank you' note.

"Not quite," the man said. "I mean, I am not your uncle. My name is Henry. Your uncle is dead, I'm afraid. Were you two close?"

"No."

"I'm sorry you had to find out this way."

Elliot looked to James for an explanation.

James hesitated, as if considering whether or not it was worth it to try and mince words.

"Henry is... a demon. Like me."

"Actually," Henry said defensively, "we are nothing alike."

James rolled his eyes. "Thank *God.*"

"Watch your tongue in front of the boy." Henry clucked his tongue, stepping closer to Elliot. He strutted, flashing like a peacock in front of his new audience. "I entered a contract with your aunt, and the price was your poor uncle's soul. I wanted hers, but I settled for second best."

Elliot was still having a hard time wrapping his head around this, and the drug burning in his veins was making every word harder to process. "...Why are you telling me this?"

"Because it is vital that you know the truth, if you are going to be of any use to us." Henry said with an uncharacteristic amount of patience. "A lot has occurred whilst you were abed. Deals were made."

"Deals? Wait. You started a contract with Aunt Violet, but you took Uncle William's soul instead?" Elliot's thoughts were catching up to him. He turned an accusatory glare towards James. "You did not tell me *that* was an option!"

James shrugged. "You didn't ask."

Elliot was not pleased with this information at all. "I could think of at least a dozen souls to feed you other than mine!"

"Could you?" Henry's eyes sparkled. "And how about a dozen more?"

It was his turn to receive the full wrath of Elliot's dark scowl.

"What are you getting at?" the young man snapped.

"A demonic contract cannot be dissolved," Henry began.

"Not without angelic interference," James interrupted.

"...Right." Henry waved his hand airily. "Your petition has to be notarized by a Dominion before it even sees the eyes of Seraph...and then there is something about cleansing and baptism... trust me, you don't want to deal with it. Far easier to sign away as many souls as possible in order to stave off your own death."

Elliot sighed, rubbing his sore eyes – which he was starting to develop a headache behind. "I'm following."

"There are *two* types of demonic contract, and I had to triple-check with James to be sure you signed the right one before we could proceed. There is one form of contract that states you must forfeit your soul when your desired goal is met. So, let's say you wanted to kill the king."

"All right." Elliot nodded.

"So James is at your side through the entire process of plotting and execution, and he makes certain you succeed. Well, when the king is dead – boom, that's it. You are dead, James consumes your soul and everyone in Hell breaks for lunch."

"Sure."

"The *other* type of contract states that your soul is not forfeit until your life reaches its natural end. So in our hypothetical situation, after you kill the king, you can seize the throne and reign for sixty years before dying and having to give up your soul." Henry tossed his hair away from his face, jittery with excitement. "You have signed a contract that will end at the same time as your natural life."

"Did I do that on purpose?" Elliot honestly could not remember.

"No," James muttered, "it was just what I had in my pocket."

"*Look,*" Henry was dying to get to the point. "We are trying to make you an offer, here! Do you know how long your natural life is meant to extend?"

"Less than a year," Elliot said. "That is all I know."

"Three months," Henry informed him brutally.

Elliot was stunned into silence. His fingers knotted in the white sheets of his bed, but his entire body felt like it was going numb.

Three months.

Three months to see the world, to run a company, to have his heart broken, to see his father die before him. Three months to have a life.

Depression crushed his chest, making his next breath hurt.

"You can't mean it," Elliot finally spoke, his voice strained.

"He does," James said disconcertedly. "I am not allowed to tell you before the contract is signed."

"Three months doesn't even make this entire thing *worth it.*" Elliot clenched his fists even tighter, setting his teeth on edge.

"I know," Henry said vivaciously, refusing to lose his zest. "But we could make everything worth it. Do you know what happens when you give your soul up to a demon?"

Elliot shook his head. Anything further he wanted to say was stuck fast in is throat.

"You get the remaining years of their life tacked on to yours." Henry paused to let that sink in. "Think about it. Twenty, thirty, *sixty* years at a time. With enough souls, Elliot, you could live…"

"Forever," Elliot said, his voice hardening.

"Well, no. But for a very, very long time." Henry extended his hand to Elliot. "It's worth it, isn't it? You don't even have to think about it very hard. The answer is obvious."

Elliot's brow crinkled. "But the contract has been signed. How can it be amended?"

"We have a guy." Henry winked. "He takes care of the pesky details."

Elliot still did not accept Henry's offered hand. "Is Aunt Violet going to get the same deal?"

Henry lifted an eyebrow. "Well it depends on how nice she is to me when I call upon her next, but my intention is to offer it to her. It would make things run a hell of a lot smoother."

Elliot lingered on the thought only a moment longer. He acted as though he had a concern, but in the end he just thrust his hand forward and took hold of Henry's in a tight grasp.

"Thorny details," Elliot said with a smile. "It can all be hashed out later."

"Most certainly," James responded, able to breathe at last in relief. "There is always later."

Violet Clifton was in need of rescue, and the croquet mallet she was holding was beginning to look like her only means of escape.

Lucy Dosett absolutely adored croquet. She had begged her sister for a match. After breakfast, Violet had taken her time changing into something suitable, hoping that if she dawdled long enough her sister might forget. But fortune was not on her side as she descended the staircase and was greeted by Lucy, gaily dressed and faintly resembling an ice cream cone in an enormous hat. Four hours later, and her luck had not really changed.

Far worse than being forced to play a game she hated was consistently *losing*.

"Oh, sister!" Lucy laughed, far too pleased with her own ability to whack a ball through a striped arch. "Perhaps we should play doubles during the next round? You will need your William to come save you!"

Lucy had repeated that exact sentence three times in the past hour. Violet was probably going to kill her.

"I am not much for croquet." Violet usually required some sort of intellectual stimulation to keep the blood in her brain flowing. "But I can understand why it would appeal to you."

"Are you not in love with our set?" Lucy sighed, ignoring everything her sister said as usual. "No one else has such beautiful steel-capped mallets."

"I imagine they could inflict some damage."

"Hiram's whole business is steel, you know," Lucy continued, tapping a pastel pink ball and watching it roll lazily across the trimmed lawn. "I don't know much about it but I thought, how wonderful for our guests, to be able to sample for themselves a taste of my husband's accomplishments."

"I suppose the steamships are never enough," Violet replied dryly.

"Propriety, dear. I can't very well host my garden parties on a steamship." Lucy tutted.

Violet mulled over it briefly. "You could try."

"What a glorious afternoon! A fox on the prowl comes upon two of society's finest birds. Which shall he feast upon first?" Henry's voice ambled over the stretch of lawn as he leapt over a small wicket, his smile as bright and infectious as ever. Violet had never been so relieved to see him. She swung her mallet from her fingertips and tapped a powder blue ball. It spun across the lawn and stopped at the toe of his shoe. He looked down at it first then back up at her, sliding his hand into his pockets.

"It appears as though I have interrupted something important."

"Where have you been?" Violet lifted her chin, setting the head of her mallet on the ground and crossing her small hands over the pommel.

"Genuflecting before an altar and weeping over my sins. The priest at confession this morning recommended it."

"Oh!" Lucy placed her hand to her chest approvingly. "I did not know you were such a devoutly religious man."

"I love church," Henry said piously.

"William," Violet spoke poisonously through her teeth, latching on to her false husband by his arm. "I would have liked to have joined you. Why did you not seek me out sooner?"

"Many apologies, my dear." He set a hand on top of hers. "I knew that you have missed your sister so and would never dream of pulling you away from each other's company."

Violet tightened her grip on his arm. Her mallet would do wonders for straightening out that slightly crooked nose...

"Oh, we have had the most splendid morning together!" Lucy said enthusiastically, sidling up to Henry. "Although Violet, my poor sister, is absolutely hopeless with a croquet mallet. I was hoping you might humor us with a game, and even out the odds?" The questioning lilt in her voice, the irritating upward inflections, and her simpering doe-eyed expression was making Violet physically sick on her stomach.

"As greatly as I desire to join your fun and salvage my wife's dignity, I fear I must whisk her away from you instead." Henry stooped a bow, lifting Lucy's hand to his lips. "I reassure you that I shall return her with haste. May I owe you a game?"

"Well." Lucy turned her cheek coyly. "You seem to be a man of honor. I expect you will uphold your word."

"I always repay my debts, madame." He bowed again and squeezed Violet's hand. "Are you ready, my dear?"

"Let's go," Violet said quietly. Henry nodded and swept away with her on his arm. Neither of them spoke until they were out of earshot. He whisked her into the garden, behind the trimmed hedges, and they vanished into the primroses.

When she was certain they were alone, she pulled her arm away from his and boxed him across the ear.

"Shit!" he hissed under his breath, ducking his head belatedly.

"You left me alone!" she snapped.

"I wasn't aware we were in enemy territory," he murmured.

"I have endured four hours of croquet."

"My deepest apologies."

"You are not sorry at all." She raised her hand to hit him again.

He threw up his arms. "I yield! You know, if you keep it up, this face will be bruised beyond recognition and I will be forced to resume my other form. And then there will be questions."

She rolled her eyes and snorted in exasperation. "I have barely touched you."

"*That* is a matter of opinion." He straightened.

"The contract has been sealed." She reached into her bag, pulling out a fragile fan and snapping it open, fluttering it in front of her face to create a small breeze. "Hasn't it?"

"Yes." He nodded.

"So we can return home."

"Ah…" He sucked on his teeth. "Not quite."

Her small breeze was turning into a small cyclone. He was growing concerned she might dislocate her wrist. "Why not?"

"We ran into a snag." He reached out, plucking up a red and yellow primrose and rolling the delicate stem between his fingers until it was reduced to pulp. "I'm being audited."

"Audited?" Her fan paused mid-air. "By … Hell? What does that even mean for you?"

"It is complicated." He rubbed his face, crumpling the primrose in his other fist. "Did you know that Elliot already has a demon with claim on his soul?"

Her eyes widened. "No."

"Neither did I," he said blandly.

"What does that mean for us?" She tilted her head, tipping her fan to rest on her chest.

"*Normally* it would mean that the first demon to lay claim – meaning his doctor, James – would get to devour the soul, and the other – meaning me – would get chained to the floor of Hell for a thousand years." He paused, amending, "Well, that is how it *used* to be. The rules may have changed. Maybe now they just stick you in the Circumlocution office for a while and make you file papers for a few centuries."

"Normally," she repeated. "Implying that something has changed?"

"Yes. An Unchaste appeared…"

"A what?"

He sighed heavily.

"A fallen angel, usually a Dominion, they all have different names… I can't keep track."

"All right, all right." She waved her fan. "Continue."

"An Unchaste named Lady appeared and he presented us with the audit papers, only I convinced him to tear them up and send a note back to Hell that they were a mistake. In the process, I came up with a plan to reduce my own workload and fill my quota… a plan of which I am not unreasonably proud. It involves you signing more souls over to me. I doubt that will be a problem for you, considering you signed your own husband away without much thought."

"I will have you know," she said testily, "that I agonized over that decision."

"For as long as it took you to sign his name?" He successfully dodged another blow.

"What do I get out this, then?" she asked.

"You get to dodge eternal damnation for a bit longer. Which, considering this is all your fault to begin with…"

"*My* fault?" she demanded. "How was I supposed to know he would come with a demon already attached? Does Hell not have some procedure on *your* end to make sure this doesn't happen?"

"Does whether or not *I* followed the rules really matter?"

"Fine. Enlighten me further." She scoffed.

"However many years, months, or whatever someone has left in their natural life gets added to yours when I devour them," he said. "But only if you have their names written down on your amended contract. Lady will take care of that part."

"How does that work, exactly?"

"I don't know," he snorted. "I never read the damn training manuals."

"Is there risk?" she asked.

"Only if we get caught."

She snapped her fan open again and fluttered it anxiously, mulling the proposition over in her head. "Do I get a choice?"

"I cannot force you to sign over souls," he replied. "It's against the rules. I do know *that* much."

"That's comforting, I suppose." She looked at him. "Suppose I decide not to help you. How many years do I have left?"

"That's going from tempting into coercion," he said loftily. "And I'm *technically* not allowed to do that. But if you were to live out your natural life... you would grow no older than thirty-five."

A little of the color drained from her face.

"Ten years," she said. "That is not very long at all."

"Long enough to bear children," Henry said. "Not long enough to see them become anything."

"You assume," she said, getting off track, "that I want children."

"No. I assume you will have them, regardless."

There was some truth to that. She sighed, gripping the end of her fan tightly and tapping it rapidly against her palm.

"All right," she said. "It is madcap but… I shall do this with you. And the contracts will be sealed in the usual way? With a piece of each of the undersigned?"

"Yes." A weight lifted off his shoulders, his cheery mood rapidly returning. "It is going to be quite brilliant, you know, you cannot fathom the things we will be able to accomplish."

"For the risk we are taking," she said, "I had better die a dictator."

CHAPTER 5

Lady stared at the needlessly ornate telephone sitting in the middle of the desk. Its brass dial mocked him, reflecting his worried face. His eyes felt like sandpaper, it had been so long since he blinked. He was waiting, and trying to keep his mind clear in the interim. That part wasn't going so well.

One did not simply dial into Hell. It always made a point of being the first to call. He knew he was expecting to hear from them any minute, which did nothing to ease the knot of tension in his stomach. He had already been sitting at the desk for what seemed like hours.

He made the decision. If the phone did not ring in the next fifteen minutes, he was going to dial the emergency extension out of simple desperation.

As sure as damnation, the phone rang obnoxiously, clattering on its cradle. Lady lunged forward, wrapping his fingers around the white opalescent handle and lifting the receiver carefully, holding it up to his ear and licking his lips, unsure of exactly what to say.

"…Hello?" he croaked.

"Hello Mr. Hayward. This is Rachel from Processing. How are you today?" The voice was pleasant and female. Lady started sweating.

"Fine!" His voice cracked in a way that could only be described as prepubescent. "I'm doing fine. It is good to hear from you, Rachel. I hope things are going nicely for you."

"Busy as always, Mr. Hayward. We received your paperwork."

"Oh! Good. I was hoping it had gone through." He swallowed hard.

"You can imagine our surprise when it appeared on our desk. We are unaccustomed to you being so prompt." She still sounded pleasant, even though she was ridiculing him. That couldn't be a good sign.

"Ah, well, you know. I've decided to get all caught up pretty recently." He rubbed the back of his neck anxiously. "…So how are the kids?"

"Mr. Hayward…"

"Yes?"

"I have a lot of calls to make."

"Right. Sorry."

"And they're doing well, thank you."

"Ah! Excellent. Glad to hear it."

"So you sent back the paperwork reporting that there was an error in Elliot Dosett's file. You say he has *not* been claimed by two separate demons?"

"Right." Lady wondered if they could tell he was lying. It wasn't like he had never lied before, but that was usually about insignificant things… such as whether he turned in his paperwork at all. "It turns out that James

Highmore actually has claim on Elliot's soul while Henry Wickes had laid claim on Violet Clifton, the aunt. The two souls in question are related so that... might explain the mix-up." It was weak, he knew it. She'd see through it in a second.

"I see." She did not sound convinced, worsening his fears. "Hell does not usually make mistakes."

"I am...painfully well aware."

"We would like for you to stay on with these contracts and see them through," the female voice continued. "Follow up on your own assessment and make certain you are one hundred percent positive in your report. These things can escalate into very serious situations, you know."

Oh yes. He knew. He had seen far too many of them slide across his desk, the unfortunate names blotted out with coffee stains.

"I will do exactly that." He continued to lie through his teeth. "And I will update you every step of the way."

"See that you do, Mr. Hayward. Have a nice day." The phone clicked, and the line went dead. It buzzed in his ear, and he set the phone down carefully, as if it might explode in his hand.

Which wasn't too much of a stretch, it had happened before.

Lady set his arms down on the desk and let his head sink, moaning into the wool sleeves of his exquisite coat. He didn't know how he had let himself get into this situation. Now he was in too deep... and there was no way out.

A thought popped up. He lifted his head and reached out for the receiver again, picking it up gingerly and holding it again to his ear as he pressed his fingers into the circles of the dial, rotating it and the pulling back to release.

6.6.6. ext. 4.

Some things were just better left to the obvious.

He sat back in the chair, pushing his tongue into his cheek as he waited for anyone to answer. The phone gave him five solid, long rings before his own voice spoke back to him, "Hello, you have reached the office of Meriwether L. Hayward…"

"Dammit!" he growled. Of course his useless intern was not going to answer the goddamn phone. Where the hell had he learned *that* sort of behavior?

The answering machine beeped. Lady tried to keep his composure and not sound like a raving lunatic over the phone.

"Listen, you no good gallivanting charlatan. You had better be sitting on your ass in that office and ignoring me. I swear to his Infernal Majesty that if you are out doing anything remotely interesting without me you are going to find yourself neck-deep in a lake of ice." He took a deep breath. Perhaps 'composure' was not his strong point under duress. "Look, I've run into some unexpected … events with the demons up here. I'll tell you all about it later but if Processing calls, or Management, or just … *anyone*... don't pick up the phone. I don't know why I'm bothering to tell you this because you clearly have no intention of doing so anyway. But just in case…"

The answering machine cut him off. A brusque reminder that brevity was not his strength, either.

He slammed the phone back down this time, annoyed at himself and his intern. Usually Francis was a sitting duck for Lady's bad moods; now he would have to find new prey if he wanted to spread it around.

Oh well, at least there were two demons to victimize.

"Hiram Dosett."

"That is the first name on your list?" James was only making half an effort to seem interested as he shook out one of Elliot's daytime coats, a nice dark blue wool.

"I thought about saving him for last," Elliot said, adjusting the tie around his throat. "Then I realized he is my best starting point."

"As you say." James slid the coat over his master's arms and Elliot shrugged it forward, adjusting it over his chest. "In order to make the contract work, you are going to have to set a modest goal, one that can be easily met in order for us to claim and devour his soul."

"Simple enough." Elliot said. "What would be sufficient? Could it be as simple as helping me kill him, and then you two claim his soul?"

"Yes," James responded. "It could be that simple... but I did not think you would want it to be."

"I should be conservative with this first strike," Elliot said, more to himself than to James before adding, "And no one said his *manner* of death had to be clean."

James adjusted his glasses, stepping back to make certain the air tank was secure on the back of the wheelchair. "Very true. How do you intend to get the first drop of his blood?"

"Your pardon?" Elliot asked, adjusting to make himself more comfortable in his seat before James grasped the handles.

"His blood," James cooed. "You know, you have to have at least a drop … to make the contract official."

Elliot pursed his lips. "I will figure it out. I don't think it should be too difficult."

"Perhaps you will figure it out at breakfast this morning."

"Perhaps."

"Lucy Dosett," Violet said with far too much relish as she set her fine-toothed comb down on top of the vanity.

"An excellent decision." Henry was standing behind her, reflecting his blonde appearance - rather the feigned one of her deceased husband – in the mirror. "I support it wholeheartedly."

"I bear her no ill will. And she is my sister." Violet slid another pin into her hair, securing the tight twist resting high on the back of her head. "But the world does not benefit in any way from her existence."

"I dare say it might breathe a little easier upon being relieved of her." He pulled a separate pin loose, just to be contrary.

She reached up and swatted his hand away, pushing the pin back into place. "Stop that. Are you ready to go to breakfast?"

"I was ready half an hour ago." He extended his hand to her, which she accepted, using it as leverage to stand in her heavy skirts.

"Forgive me for caring," she said sardonically, releasing his hand as soon as she was steady and sweeping austerely across the room, headed for the door. She paused as soon as she reached it, her hand going towards the knob. She felt his fingers brush over the back of her hand, and his body pressed against hers from behind, nearly pinning her between him and the dark chestnut wood. Her breath caught in her throat, her entire body freezing.

"No hesitation," Henry whispered, his lips close to her ear, brushing over the shell. "No regrets."

"None," she said breathily. "I am resolute."

His name was Yahweh, El Shaddai, Elohim, and Jehovah Jireh. He had a dozen other names as well, tucked in the crinkled, water-stained pages of Bibles that sat yellowing on a middle class suburban bookshelf, wedged snugly between a child's encyclopedia and an outdated dictionary. He had a few more, usually on reserve for being chanted by priests – however many of *those* were still around.

He was God the Father, God the Son, God who hadn't lost a round of golf since he picked it up in 1589.

Of course, Michael was determined to see that change.

"You can't make it," the archangel crowed, leaning on his caddy cart with perfectly tanned ankles smugly crossed.

God rested the side of his club against the ground, gauging the distance with hawk-like brown eyes. "Shut your trap."

Michael smirked and did not respond, adjusting the curved bill of his white cap so that it shaded his nose a fraction better, as if he ever burned or freckled.

God lifted his golf club and pulled it backwards, building up momentum for the swing.

"Lord!"

The club bit into rich sod, unearthing a hunk of grass that went flying into the air, minus the golf ball he had actually been aiming for. God set his straight white teeth and shot a look at Michael, who simply shrugged.

"It wasn't me." The archangel tossed a casual glance over his shoulder. "Although Uriah seems to be holding something on the tip of his tongue."

"Remind me which one Uriah is, again?" God reached down to straighten the tee his ball was sitting on.

"Uriel's younger brother, he just got promoted to supervisor in the Deportation Department."

"Marvelous."

"Lord!" Uriah called again as he approached, pausing to try and catch his breath, doubling over so that his hands rested on his knees. "I'm sorry to interrupt, Lord, but we just received a fax from Hell…"

"Hell still uses fax?" God asked.

"I didn't even know *we* still had a fax machine," Michael chirped.

"There are one or two left around here. Clunky old hunks of machinery but they get the job done." Uriah straightened, waving a yellow manila envelope. Michael took it from him and pinched the clip, sliding the papers out and into his waiting hand.

"These are our deportation papers," the archangel said.

"Ah. Yes. Clipped to the *front...*" Uriah took the stack and slipped off the paperclip, shuffling the papers around until a cleaner set was sitting on top. "This is a statement from Hell, saying several centuries ago we sent them a Fallen angel who was not properly documented. They want the reason for his Fall, statements from at least three Seraphim confirming witness of "hellish" behavior at separate intervals, they want a copy of his evaluation of corruption, and they want the Almighty's signatures all over the place." He looked apologetically at God. "I'm sorry sir. Something must have gotten lost when we moved offices. Usually every Fallen is processed perfectly before being sent down below..."

God waved his hand as if none of it mattered. "Just see that it gets done. I will sign whatever I need to. Now, if you would be so kind...?" He lifted a nicely shaped eyebrow.

Uriah blushed and straightened out his necktie. "Of course! I'll get right on it." He vanished immediately, and God wondered why he hadn't done that to make his entrance in the first place.

"He forgot the paperwork," Michael said, still looking over the stack. "I'll return them to him after the game."

"That's fine," God said, already lining up his club again.

"Meriwether Hayward. I don't remember him."

God's club nicked the top of the ball. It went spinning off the tee and into the dirt a few inches away. An Almighty glare compelled it to continue rolling until it fairly bounced into the hole.

He remembered Meriwether. He remembered him all too well.

CHAPTER 6

Lucy dragged her heavy eyelids open and was greeted by a hundred flickering flames - whale oil lamps meretriciously blazing in the darkness. They were the burning glares of magistrates behind glistening glass curves, elegant brass foundations burnished to an unnatural gleam. Lucy had never realized she could be surrounded by so much warm, yellow light and yet feel so cold.

She tried to move, but the only thing she successfully managed to lift was her head. Her arms were above her head, crossed at the wrists and tied tightly to what was probably the leg of her wardrobe. She tried to move her legs, but she could not feel them at all. Panic fluttered in her chest and she tugged on her arms again, whimpering helplessly, tilting her head back further to try and look past the lamps. All she could see was a dim outline of the vaulted roof. Of course... because she was on the floor.

She wanted to scream, but she was afraid to even speak.

A weight settled on her hips. Only when she felt the brush of fabric against her skin did she realize she was naked.

Lucy opened her mouth to scream, but she barely got a squeak out before a soaked rag was stuffed into her mouth. It tasted bitter like alcohol and made her choke. A thousand small cuts on her dry lips burned as she made a face and tried to spit the offending object out, but there was too much of it – and the interaction with her tongue made it worse.

"Shh." Violet's voice, and gentle fingers touched Lucy's cheek. "Or I will set it on fire."

Lucy made an indistinct sound around her gag and hot tears welled up; partially the bright lights, partially the fumes from the alcohol... mostly the terrible sense of betrayal.

"I know," Violet said. "Just remember that I love you, and we will always be sisters." She touched the tip of a sharp penknife to the hollow of Lucy's throat. "Even if your twenty-seven years on this earth were a waste of hot air."

The edge of the blade bit into supple skin, breaking it apart like ripe fruit and sinking into the fat underneath. Blood and bodily oils rose to the surface, streaming down porcelain skin in dark crimson rivulets.

"The contract," Henry said. "Before she dies."

Violet paused, distracted, nodding. "Yes." She swirled her fingertips in the blood, lifting her hand and pressing them against the paper that he held out for her, somewhere underneath where she had signed Lucy's name. She had already given her own blood to the contract. When he folded it up, it crumbled into ash, and then he stepped back – allowing her to continue. His blue eyes were bleeding orange, bright as floodlights from the shadows where he stood. He watched her, rapaciously dragging his tongue over his lips, flicking the tip over his pointed incisors. His turn was coming.

Violet ignored her sister's sounds as she dragged the knife down between Lucy's flat, wilting breasts. She pushed it deeper with every inch, feeling the resistance of muscle all the way down to the abdomen. Heat and acrid-smelling gases hit Violet in the face, telling her she that she had probably nicked something she hadn't meant to quite yet. Ah, well.

Violet dipped her knife into the fresh slit, spearing something. She lifted it out, her hand partially coated in blood, pulling out a length of slimy pale intestine.

She used her other hand to grip it, drawing more of it out. It just kept coming … seemingly endless. She started getting tired of it after only a few tugs. They were heavy and steaming and smelled ghastly. Disgusted, she raised her knife, finding it harder to keep a proper grip as she leaned over her sister's body. Scalding blood soaked through her thin bloomers and stockings – all she was wearing, besides her corset – and she searched Lucy for any lingering signs of life.

There was a fragile heartbeat, a frightened little thing beating its wings inside the jugular. Violet tilted her head, and stuck her knife straight into the artery. Blood sprayed over her face and chest as she dragged the knife only halfway across Lucy's small neck before the knife slipped out of her hands and Violet swore, leaning back and shoving sticky strands of dark hair out of her face.

Lucy's throat gaped half-open in a mangled leer, gurgling blood and hissing for a few wet breaths before finally giving up.

"There," Violet said, her voice coming out hoarse. "It's done…"

Henry could not restrain himself any longer. He dropped to his knees and straddled Lucy's face, sitting opposite Violet, and dug his fingers into the opening on the small woman's chest. Violet forced herself to watch as he pulled apart the ribcage, Lucy's chest buckling and her spine snapping with the preternatural force. He ripped out the heart and held it, dripping, in his hand while he stared down at the soul, his smile wide and his eyes casting spotlights on the shallow cavity behind it – what seemed like a thousand pearls, quivering like jelly.

He discarded the heart carelessly. It hit the floor with a heavy wet smack. Henry scooped his hand tenderly into the dip, the cradle of sinew and bone, and herded half of the soul's little pearls into his palm. He brought his head down and crammed them all in his mouth, shameless of his gluttony, as juices gushed between his fingers and permeated the air with a sickly sweet smell – like dying rose petals and chocolate.

The demon devoured his portion of the soul like a starving child, tilting back his head when he was finished and sucking the remnants from his fingertips.

His eyes were blue again.

Violet sucked in a shallow breath, her heart felt like it was struggling to beat.

"…You only ate half," she said softly.

84

"James," Henry said, leaning over the body and pressing his hands against the floor, his face now inches away from hers.

"Oh." She looked him up and down. His face was smeared with the clear, viscous liquid. "…What does it taste like?"

"Like…" He paused. "Turkish delight." He rose up on his knees, taking her face in his, and claiming her lips in a demanding kiss.

Violet seized hold of his shirt, knotting her fingers in the fabric, pulling him closer. His hands slipped around her neck up into her hair, pulling out pins and shaking it loose until it fell around her hair in soft mink waves. He dragged his tongue down her throat, sliding the tip over her collarbone before pressing his hungry mouth against the swell of her breasts, his hands gripping her corseted waist. He held her close to him as he took in mouthfuls of soft, perfumed flesh and drew it into his mouth, leaving behind red marks that would with time fade to purple.

He pulled up on her breasts, just enough to get the creamy flesh above the rim of the corset, exposing round, dark nipples. He flickered his tongue over their tips before sucking. They hardened in his mouth, and over his own panting he heard her long, low moans as she pushed her fingers into his hair and tilted her head back.

"I want you," was all she said. She did not need to say more. He cupped his hands around her ass and squeezed, his fingers ripping at the laces of her bloomers yanking them down her hips. He dragged his fingernails down the prominent V of her sharp hip bones, disappearing between her legs and touching the vulva, enshrined in dark pubic hair, and then the wet entrance, already expanding and eager to sink down onto his fingers.

Two of his fingers slid inside and he drew them back and forth, slowly, feeling her hips undulate and her breath quicken, her cheeks flushing. He pulled his fingers out entirely, dragging them over the length of her slit and rubbing the thick secretion over her clit, drawing more needy sounds from her throat.

She kissed him again, and then he urged her to turn around. He slid his hands up her back, over the rough laces of her corset, and grabbed hold of her hair, pushing her down so that her palms were against the floor. He unbuttoned his pants, dragging them down his hips and pulling is cock free, sliding the tip up and down the ridges of her labia – her wetness gathering on his head and driving him crazy with desire.

He held on to her hips, pushing his cock inside, torturously slow. She groaned and sank closer to the floor. He leaned over until his chest was pressed to her back and drew his hips back only a little before making his first thrust – so overwhelmed by pleasure he felt like he was close to bursting immediately.

The silence around them was filled only by his short, erratic breaths – her barely restrained whimpers – the sound of his wet flesh smacking into hers.

His thrusts slowed and he pressed closer to her, making an inhuman sound as he grabbed her breasts and burst inside of her. She shuddered and sighed, but gasped again when he reached underneath her – staying inside while he stroked her clit once more – swift, deep circular motions. She bit her lip and cried out as she orgasmed, pushing herself down onto his softening cock as the warmth of her own climax trickle down her thighs.

He kissed her cheek and her delicate shoulder, pulling back and sitting again on his knees – his cock wet and limp again between his legs as he swept back his hair and pulled up his pants. She took another minute to catch her breath and bask in the sensation before straightening up as well, finding her bloomers and pulling them back on, lacing them around her waist.

"I think," she said, gathering all of her soft brown hair in one hand and pulling it over her shoulder. "We should figure out what to do with the body."

"That won't be an issue," he said. "Lady will help. Oh…" He turned around, setting one hand on Lucy's head. Two of his fingers settled against her eye, pulling the eyelids as far open as they could go, and with his other hand he dug his fingers into either corner, plucking the eyeball out of her head like a berry before doing the same to its twin.

"There." He rolled them around in his palm like a grisly pair of dice. "He will want these. Does your sister have something I can put these in, or…?"

Still slightly disoriented, drowsy and satiated as she was, Violet stood and ventured around the room, eventually located a beaded black handbag that she handed over to him.

Henry opened up the clutch and dropped the eyes inside. He scooped up the remainder of Lucy's soul and added that to the mixture before closing the handbag and standing up.

"I need to change," Violet said, looking down at her blood-soaked bloomers.

"Would you like me to help?" He winked lasciviously.

She paused, looking him up and down, and then gave him the first real smile he had ever seen flicker over her lips.

"Yes," she said, and turned, presenting her back to him. "Help me with this corset."

He grinned, setting the handbag down on the vanity. He walked over to her, stepping over her sister's corpse as he did so. He pinched the corset strings, settling his free hand on her cinched waist, and gave the strings a sharp tug.

He leaned in close, touching his lips to her neck. "Of course, my dear."

The first thing Hiram noticed when he regained consciousness was that he could not move. He tried to shrug his shoulders and pull back his arms, but each attempt at motion was met by the restraints of thick, heavy cloth. His arms were wrapped tightly across his chest, his hands pinned to his sides. A series of intricate buckles kept everything in place. It took his brain several minutes slogging through a drug-induced fog to realize he was in a straitjacket.

"I apologize," James said, and Hiram head the buckles move. "Is that too loose?" The arms of the jacket tightened until he felt his circulation being cut off. Hiram made an irate, strangled sound and James smiled, stepping back to his medical case.

"What is the meaning of this?" Hiram felt like he was out of breath just by having so much pressure against his abdomen.

"You have become a liability." Elliot's soft words sounded strained, as if he had scripted this entire scene. Hiram could barely make out the shadowy outline of his son in the darkness of the small office. His only reassurance that Elliot was, in fact, in the room was the consistent puffing of the respirator. "I have the rest of the family to think about. I know it is difficult to grasp now but give it some time. You will come to understand."

"Why are you doing this?" Hiram was almost too confused to be fearful. He struggled against the straitjacket knowing it was futile, his sense of alarm increasing with each severe metal clank that rose from James' medical bag. "Elliot. Listen to me. *Look at me.* Let me go. And we can talk this through."

"No, Father." Elliot's voice was steel. "Look at *me.*"

Hiram felt compelled to meet Elliot's flinty, hateful eyes.

"I want to be the last thing you see," Elliot said steadily, lifting his chin. "James."

Hiram's world went pitch black in an instant. Unbearable pain incised his entire skull as he felt what could have been small tapered spoons, delicately handled, gouge into his eyes.

He screamed, wanting to thrash but finding he could not. He could feel hot, thick blood pouring down his cheeks. Whatever drugs they had given him worked alongside the pain to make him dizzy. When the spoons were pulled free, his head lolled grotesquely, in danger of passing out.

"Elliot would have loved to do everything himself," James said. Hiram could barely hear him over the din of his own screams, still ringing in his ears, as well as the blood roaring past. "But his physical condition will simply not allow for it. I hope you understand."

"Why?" Hiram's breath came out a harsh wheeze.

"Well because he cannot very well move out of that chair for one…"

Hiram knew that James knew that that was not what he meant at all.

Elliot wasn't much for dramatic speeches, elaborating exactly all Hiram had done to him to warrant this end. He felt vaguely insulted that his father did not already *know*. It should have been obvious. All that Elliot had been through, that they had discussed…

No, if Hiram didn't already know, Elliot wasn't going to explain it … however condescendingly.

Hiram heard what sounded like wood smacking against a fleshy palm. There was a dreadful pause left hanging in the air – an end so close, he could taste the blood in his mouth already.

"I think," Elliot said, his words still sounding like a strange echo of things dredged up before, "that you look like you could use some rest."

The dull pain did not last long, though the sound of the sharp crack lingered with him until he died – which, unfortunately, was not immediate.

James was not satisfied with the first swing. Hiram's body slumped forward with the force, his head landing on the surface of his work desk. James pursed his lips and lifted the steel-capped mallet again, bringing it down once more again the back of Hiram's head. The second blow was more devastating than the first, caving in the entire back of the skull. It crackled like an eggshell, fragments of glistening bone jutting from the grisly wound. The mess inside resembled the pulp of a melon.

"That's why we took the eyes first," James said, already feeling better about the outcome. "Lady likes them whole."

Elliot wrinkled his nose. "Get the rest of it over with quickly."

James sighed. He rolled up his sleeve delicately, taking a moment to flex his fingers as if he was not going to enjoy this. He reached in through the cavity made by the mallet, his hand travelling down the throat and hitting the ribcage. He moved his fingers around until he felt them slide into the groove behind the heart. Crooking his fingers, he scooped out all of the soul he could find – they came out in the form of round, jelly-like balls iridescent blue in color. He poured some into his other hand until he had an equal amount in both. Then he placed the first handful into the same box as Hiram's eyes while popped the other handful into his mouth.

He closed his mouth around them and bit down. Juices spurted from the sides of his mouth. Horrified, he whipped out a handkerchief and dabbed at them, choking a bit as he recovered himself and swallowed.

"How...dainty," Elliot said dryly.

James ignored him with the exception of a fleeting glare, straightening himself up again after re-gathering his composure. Elliot was looking at the remnants of the soul curiously. Unable to help himself, he reached out and picked up one of the balls between his fingertips.

James said nothing. He watched the boy, his expression strangely blank. The ball was a little firmer than it looked like it might be. Elliot squished it between his fingertips, but it did not burst. He looked at James, as if thinking the demon would stop him, and then popped the ball into his mouth.

It broke apart on contact with his tongue, searing his mouth with its juices like boiling water. Elliot screamed, spitting out as much of it as he could. It felt like fire squeezing between his teeth. He panted, waving his hand for something to drink while his body jerked spasmodically, tugging against the tubes of his respirator. Fearing for the tubes, James quickly brought him something cool to drink. Luckily there had been a pitcher of water nearby.

Elliot swallowed the water and asked for more. James patiently provided him with a second cup. Elliot fell against the back of his wheelchair, his breathing pained. He looked up at James accusingly.

"Why didn't you stop me?" the young man demanded.

James shrugged. "I wanted to see what would happen."

"Does it not burn *your* mouth?" Elliot tilted his head back to drain the last few drops of water lingering in the bottom seams.

"No. It tastes wonderful. Cold and sweet like…" He paused to try and think of a proper comparison. "Like jelly babies!"

Elliot snorted. "Jelly babies from hell, maybe."

"Exactly!"

Elliot rolled his eyes in exasperation and handed back the cup, putting his hands on his wheelchair.

"We have a body to dispose of. Are we supposed to meet your auditor, after this?"

"Yes, to deliver the eyes. And Henry and I will exchange the split souls."

"You enjoy them," Elliot said, still regretting everything that had led up to his tasting even one bead.

"Oh..." James' eyes sparkled behind his glasses. "We will."

CHAPTER 7

You couldn't just eat an eye any old way you pleased. There was a method.

The way demons devoured souls was an atrocity. They just crammed the entirety in their mouth, or as much as they could hold at one time, and gobbled it down as if it was the last meal they would ever eat. They never took the time to savor. Lady had never tasted a soul, but with all of those little bubbles, he imagined you could eat two or three at a time, sucking away the sweetness and the thin film that kept them all clinging together before biting into them. Demons ran on the impulsive seizure of momentary pleasures, and they applied that even to their eating habits. Watching a demon go down on a soul was like watching a starving dog tear into a carcass and it was *disgusting*.

Eyes were different. You had to *appreciate* them. Many just popped the entire thing in their mouth and swallowed without chewing…but that was no way to live.

With a sharp little penknife, Lady made a thin incision down the side, where the excess tissue was pinkest. He had rinsed away all of the blood and fuzzies gathered from being tossed around handbags and velvet-lined boxes and now he just held four whole, perfect eyes. He placed his mouth to the incision, sucking out the cold, thick goo from its center. The jelly of the eye was arguably the best part. Many complained that it didn't taste like anything but Lady disagreed. He loved it. To him it tasted cool and slightly sweet – like a cucumber. He squeezed the eyeball until every last drop was out and then opened it up all the way, turning it inside out and running his tongue over the black insides, finally grabbing one end with his teeth and pulling the outside in half. Eyes were chewy, unsurprisingly, and he loved the texture of them against his teeth. He popped the other half into his mouth happily picked up another in the meantime, already slicing in.

"I don't know how you can do that." Henry cringed. "They are fat and gross."

"I don't like the pink part." James wrinkled his nose. "It's all flabby and slimy."

Lady sniffed. "Charlatans. Both of you."

"It doesn't even taste like anything." Henry had already finished his share of Hiram's soul and was now stretched out in a chair, lounging like a particularly idle cat.

"You could at least salt it," James said, slumping in his seat with his cheek resting against his fingers, curled inwardly towards his palm.

"Everyone has their own taste," Lady said, looking to see the color of the iris before he sucked the eye into his mouth. In his opinion, all of the colors tasted different. "I knew an Unchaste who liked to eat brains. I think brains are heavy and dense but he loved them. He said each memory had a flavor. Just goes to show." He shrugged and reached for another eye.

Violet stood by the fireplace, catty-corner to Elliot, who was drumming his fingers against the arms of his wheelchair. Lady had not found either of them to be very interesting people upon their introduction. Elliot was too solemn. People who took themselves that seriously usually died of brain aneurysms before they were forty. Violet was too aloof. It was easy to tell she thought highly of herself. And if there was one thing Lady couldn't stand, it was unwarranted arrogance present in anyone other than himself.

Humans had always been like that. He usually found them difficult to deal with. He never understood a demon's propensity for finding them so delightful.

Maybe it was the smell of the souls that drew them closer. Like hounds to a bitch in heat.

It was a theory.

Lady finished his meal and settled back in his chair, feeling sated for the first time in what seemed like forever. He picked up his glass and sniffed it, a nice Pinot Noir. He sipped it daintily, feeling their gazes harden as they became aware he was stalling. They assumed it was dramatic effect.

Really, he was thinking.

"How long do we intend to keep this up?" He finally set his glass down, watching the remnants of the delectable red slide down the sides and pool at the center.

"However long we can," Henry said. "*I* do not intend to get caught."

"In the scope of eternity," Lady said, "'Forever' is a moot point."

"Are you going to submit the paperwork?" James glanced nervously at the sealed contracts, each bearing Lady's stamp of approval.

"I have to," Lady said. "But I'm going to let it sit for a few weeks. I have to make my activity seem *realistic*. If I start turning things in on time consistently, they're going to know something is wrong."

"And your reports...?"

"Those will probably end up conveniently lost underneath my coffee mugs." Lady adjusted his glasses prudishly. "Really, James. You have no faith in my ability to prevaricate."

"None whatsoever," James said. "I have no faith in anything at all."

"That's what makes a demon, I suppose." Lady cast a glance towards Henry. "And how about you, sir?"

"I'm sorry?" Henry looked at him, blue eyes blinking slowly.

"What has rendered you so blessedly quiet?" Lady tilted his head.

Henry drummed his fingers against his knee and smiled. "Mostly that I'm hungry."

"Insatiable." Lady scoffed. "Well." He licked the last droplets of Pinot Noir from the edge of his glass. "No use in dallying, then. Nose back to the grindstone."

"That is exactly what I was aiming to avoid," Henry said in the manner of a lazy child who does not wish to be dragged out of bed.

"Well, that's Hell for you," Lady replied. "It's just full of contradictions."

The most frequented office in Hell was 87% smog, 13% breathable atmosphere, and smelled most often of stale mints from the bottom of an old woman's purse. It was primarily because Satan smoked a lot of menthols.

The walls of Satan's office were glass, but the smoke as always so thick it was impossible to see inside. The doorknob was always warm to the touch and greasy, instantly bringing to mind the image of the millions of nervous, sweaty palms that must have grasped it in the past. Levi hesitated to grab it even now, and he was one of the few who had been known to re-emerge *alive*. Or at the very least in one piece. Satan had a fond habit of taking pieces that you didn't think you would miss until you realized you were crippled by their absence. Levi had known a demon to lose a pinky once. Nearly thirty human years later they had gone stark mad during tea time and were sent to the ninth circle for trying to gnaw off their own hand.

That was madness did to you in this place. It slowly chipped away at your psyche until you lost your shit and tried to fling teacakes at the Minister of Hell's head.

Levi clutched his folder to his chest. Taking a deep breath, he opened up the office door. Smoke rolled out in thick, curling plumes. He coughed, eyes watering as he struggled to see far enough to walk towards the desk. The room also smelled like coffee. Barely.

"Good morning, Levi." You had to give the guy credit, he had a voice like sex on a fur rug.

"Good morning sir..." Levi took half a step forward.

"Shut the door." A fresh stream of smoke spilled into the air.

Levi backpedaled. The door shut when his heel fell against it and he tried to regain some dignity. He cleared his throat, coughing again, and crushed the papers so tightly against his chest he felt like it was possible to absorb them.

"Do you have my papers for me?" Satan sounded amused. He always sounded amused, as if eternity was an empyreal joke and only he knew the punch line.

"Yes." Levi quickly closed the distance between them, setting a clipped stack of papers as well as a manila folder onto the desk. "All of what you asked for, every demonic contract from both files. As well as a list of all audits sent to Hayward's desk..."

"Thank you." Satan pinched the bottom of one of the papers, tugging it free from its clip and lifting it up until it disappeared into the smoke. His face was well-obscured. Levi wasn't entirely sure if he actually knew what his boss looked like. All he had ever been able to make out was the well-dressed torso. A nice pinstripe navy suit and a red power tie.

"Well," Satan said. "This is interesting."

'Interesting' did not sound very good at all.

"Did you also remember to check with Registration?" Satan set the paper down, and picked up the rest of the neat stack, flipping through it casually.

"Yes. There were no Elliot Dosett from the specific year you mentioned." Levi watched every movement, as if he were standing within sights of a serpent coiled to strike.

"There was no Violet Clifton, either. There *was* a William Clifton."

"And Hiram and Lucy Dosett?"

"They were registered as well. I checked with Karen, she'd never even seen the faces of Elliot or Violet. And she *never* forgets a face."

"Interesting." Satan set the stack of papers down and lifted the manila folder, opening it up to peer inside. He tipped it over and a dozen crinkled, coffee-stained papers slid out.

"You can well imagine," Levi mentioned, a touch desperately, "the trouble I had getting ahold of these."

"A job well done, to be sure. You will be commended..." Satan tapped his cigarette over an ashtray shaped and painted like a shiny red apple. His cigarette dribbled grey ash into its core. "Hayward was not in his office then, I take it."

"No, sir. Only his intern who, I might add, made an immense fuss the entire time while looking for these papers."

"Did he mention Hayward's whereabouts, or when we might expect him to return?"

"No," Levi sighed. "Not that I know of, anyway. He did an awful lot of grumbling. It was very hard to understand."

"I see." Satan set the stained pages down on top of the neater stack and leaned back in his chair, perfectly manicured fingertips touching.

"Thank you for your services here, Levi. You may return to your office."

Levi gratefully accepted the cue for his dismissal. He turned and walked out, carefully shutting the door behind him.

Satan waited for him to leave, then ground the end of his cigarette into the ashtray before pressing a gleaming gold button on his desk.

A buzzer sounded overhead. "Yes, Mr. Lucifer?" his secretary's voice rapped sharply over the line.

"Cancel my afternoon meetings," he said. "I have some paperwork to look through. Don't let anyone in. Except for the two... you know the ones."

"I do, sir," his secretary affirmed. "Very good."

The line went dead. Satan reached into the deep pocketed nestled in the lining of his blazer and pulled out a silver cigarette case.

He snapped it open and held it up to his nose, inhaling the smell of fresh tobacco and menthol.

He set the cigarette case down on the desk, and then began the impossible task of discerning Meriwether Hayward's handwriting.

PART 2 — PURGATORY

CHAPTER 8

It had been a very busy thirteen years.

Violet was still not convinced time had passed at all. It did not show in the mirror. When she looked at her reflection, she saw the same woman who had stared back at her the night William had died. All of society had noticed it. Men dropped love notes into her lap. Women asked her about her skin routine. Violet always made certain to smile politely and tell them it was strictly the blood of virgins.

They always laughed that off so easily.

She could not remember a single thing that had occurred between the ages of 25 and 38, except that somewhere in that interval five children had appeared. *Five.* Henry said they were hers. She was still trying to accept that.

Time was obviously passing. Things constantly changed around her. The monarchy had swapped hands from king to queen. Her children grew like vines; one minute clinging to her skirts, the next trying to recite poetry while their younger siblings screamed.

The world was turning, and yet her heart felt still in her chest.

They had sold the old townhouse in favor of a new one that far better accommodated a family of seven. It was joined by another, occupied frequently by Elliot on his 'business trips' into town. Lady often flitted between the two – usually wherever eyes were being harbored. He had a favorite chair by the living room fireplace where he would sit, eat, and go over his paperwork. He had gained a little weight in the past decade, resembling a classical cherubim rather than the shrewd librarian he used to. Every now and then he would mutter about how mortal earth was making him fat before popping another eyeball into his mouth.

It was all going well... far too well. Violet was always holding her breath, waiting for the other shoe to fall.

"You are far too pessimistic," Henry said, lifting the youngest, ten months old, into the air and balancing her on his hip. "Isn't she, Nellie? Mama is far too pessimistic." His voice dissolved into coos and kissing noises, a few of those kisses landing on a chubby porcelain cheek.

"It is only a matter of time before we are found out," she said, tying off the braid in her three year-old's hair with a pale pink ribbon.

"It has only been thirteen years. Do you know how small that is, in the scope of eternity?" He still wasn't looking at her, playing with baby Nellie's pouty bottom lip and grinning. "No, she doesn't. Thirteen years is nothing, mama."

"Will you stop that?" Violet asked impatiently, gently pushing on her elder daughter's shoulders to let her know she was finished. "Speak to me like an adult."

His smiled disappeared and he regarded her, sighing. "You're too paranoid."

"Perhaps I wouldn't be," she said, "if Edward were not already sprouting horns."

"Aren't they cute?" Henry asked proudly, his smile returning. "He looks like a little baby goat…"

"You didn't *tell* me that they would have *horns!*" Her lip curled. They had only had this conversation five times in the past three days.

"I thought you knew," Henry said innocently.

"Why on earth would I know that?" She rose, brushing loose hairs away from her skirt. The three year-old looked up at her father with large, owlish blue eyes.

"Am I going to get horns, papa?" she asked quietly, twisting her skirt up in her pudgy hands. Henry smiled and patted the top of her head. She squeaked and pulled away so he wouldn't mess up her braid.

"When you're older, Ettie," he said. "And maybe a tail, too!" He winked.

Violet glowered. "You had better be joking."

He outright giggled. "Maybe I am. Maybe not."

Ettie's mouth fell open in an astonished 'O' shape. "But you don't have horns! Mama doesn't either."

"Oh, I have horns sweetheart," he said. "You just can't see them right now."

The child grinned. "Horns like papa!" She ran from the room, crowing victoriously all the way down the hall.

Violet wasn't certain of where they came by all this energy… but she knew she sure would like a piece of it.

"Let him grow out his hair," Henry said dismissively, returning to the topic Violet insisted on pursuing. "That will cover them well enough."

"For how long?" She folded her arms.

"Until they fall off and bigger ones grow back, I should think." He set the baby back down on the rug, watching her crawl towards her doll and sit down, pulling it into her lap. "Think of it this way. If we are ever in dire straits we can sell them all to the circus."

"I am so glad that *you* can find it funny." She whirled away furiously, brushing past the child before it could have a chance to latch on to her skirt. "A *sensible* demon like James wouldn't have done this to me."

"He couldn't have gotten it up long enough, you're right." Henry approached her from behind, settling hands onto her shoulders and massaging his fingers deep into the knotted, tense muscles. "I adore you, you know. If I did not… none of this would affect me as it does."

"That is neither flattering nor comforting." She scoffed.

"I crave you," he said earnestly.

"I'm sure."

He bent his neck, kissing her on the soft spot behind her ear, trailing the tip of his tongue down until it slipped over her earlobe. She side and closed her eyes, succumbing to his touches, her hands coming up to rest on top of his.

It wasn't fair, how he did these things to her.

"Crave. Lust. Desire. Need," she said softly. "All words that trace their way back to *hunger*. I know you want my soul, Henry, is that why you keep me so close?"

"Love is not something demons are capable of," Henry whispered, his tongue traveling down the back of her neck, tendrils of her soft mink brown hair tickled his nose. "Hunger is as close as we can get."

She couldn't count how many times he had told her that. It stung less and less, as the years wore on.

He wasn't really worth breaking her heart over. She knew that. Had he been human rather than a rakish demon, she would have never looked twice at him after the first night.

The door burst open. Violet closed her eyes, her fingers tightening around his. The baby was easy to forget, but the older children…they made themselves as visible – and as loud – as possible at all times.

"Lady, Lady, Lady!" six year-old Emmett whooped, swinging his silk tie around in the air above his head and gamboling about in circles so that he staggered dizzily every time he tried to take a step forward. True to the declaration, Lady entered moments later. He was holding a very smug Ettie who gloated over a handful of colorful candy – a dragon over her gems.

"Who let you in here?" Henry demanded, his hands still on Violet's shoulders as his eyes swept the room for the traitor.

"I did," Emmett said imperiously, sliding a lollipop into his mouth. "He had *candy*."

"Satan knows you don't need it," Violet murmured.

"You act as though you are the one to deal with them all the time," Lady said, setting Ettie down and brushing off his gloves. "Just send them to run around their nursemaid."

"I haven't seen her all afternoon," Violet said. "I think she is crying in a closet somewhere."

"I wouldn't doubt it." Lady patted Ettie's head. She crinkled her nose and ran over to Henry, hiding behind his legs and secretively popping another candy into her mouth.

"I have come to review the month," Lady said, getting more or less straight to business, his gaze sliding between demon and noblewoman. "I'm guessing Elliot and James have not arrived yet."

"They should be here this evening," Violet said. "You are always early."

"Since you're here, will you take tea with us?" Henry invited. "We were just about to adjourn to the parlor."

Lady's gaze flickered towards Henry's bulging crotch doubtfully and he adjusted his glasses, sniffing. "Of course."

Violet shrugged Henry off her shoulders, scooping baby Nellie from the floor and handing her off to Emmett, who struggled to carry the baby almost as long as he was.

"Take your sister and go play," Violet said. "Find your nurse, wherever she might be hiding."

"Yes mama," Emmett said obediently, struggling to speak around his lolli as he tottered out of the room with one baby sister, the other following at his heels after a nudge from Henry.

"I noticed the eldest is getting his horns," Lady said conversationally as the adults started towards the parlor.

Henry groaned.

"Don't..." he began, but it was already too late.

"I knew they were obvious!" Violet sounded both validated and annoyed.

"It is a natural development at this age," Lady continued, trying to be helpful. "They look like the beginnings of ram's horns, but I suppose you won't know that for a few more years..." He was ignoring Henry's wild gestures as the demon desperately tried to motion for him to can it.

Henry eventually gave up and his arms fell against his sides.

"I have ram's horns," he said, a notable amount of pride in his voice.

"I have seen them," Lady confirmed. "They are beautiful."

"Aw!" Henry put a hand to his chest. "Lady...!"

"From a purely *structural* standpoint," the Unchaste was quick to amend. "They are far too good for you."

Henry folded his arms, appearing to pout. "You ruined it."

"Henry, you cannot be offended in the face of the truth." Violet gestured sharply to the maid setting out the tea, waving her away. The maid bobbed a curtsy and vanished from the parlor. Violet pulled out her own chair, cutting off Henry's attempt to do so first, and sat down daintily, arranging her voluminous skirts.

Lady eyed them, surveying cut and color and trying to decide whether or not he approved. He decided that he did not, and in the event that he should ever decide to present as female again, he would not chose the fashion of an old lady as his model.

"Lady." Henry voice was clipped. The demon looked at him curiously, squeezing the juices from a generously halved lemon into his tea. Lady realized he hadn't been paying attention to anything either of them had said. It still probably wasn't anything important.

"My apologies." Lady scooped a generous spoonful of white sugar into his teacup. "Were you asking me a question?"

"Does James know you are here?" Henry repeated himself. Lady scowled and stirred his tea.

"Of course not," the Unchaste said, taking a sip. "If James knew I was coming, he would not appear at all. Elliot would come down with something dreadful and they would be forced to excuse themselves. You have noticed that, haven't you? Elliot is always in perfect health for three weeks out of the month, and then for the very last he always manages to come down with something dreadful that prohibits him from leaving the house."

Henry licked the rim of his teacup snidely. "I hadn't noticed."

Elliot wore the years like a particularly nice dinner jacket. They flattered him; not hiding but rather – accentuating his finer features. Where Henry had prevented Violet from aging altogether, James had applied the years in pastry-thin layers over all the right places. He spent time drawing out sharp cheekbones and deep-set, cruel eyes. And now that Elliot was nearly the ripe age of thirty a touch of iron gray had been permitted to kiss his ink black hair. James thought it might behoove his master to appear older, especially when working so closely with his peers in the shark-infested sea of the steel industry.

Tonight they were paying their monthly visit to the Clifton Household, which would mean a trip into town. Elliot despised travel, as James had come to as well. Neither of them were going to be looking forward to that evening.

"I never like these visits," Elliot said, reiterating what James already knew. He straightened his cravat in the mirror, securing it with a cameo stickpin. "Why doesn't Lady just mail us a copy of the month's review?"

"Why do angels dance on pinheads?" James asked rhetorically, kneeling to pull Elliot's feet up onto their rests. Over the years, Elliot's health had improved so that he no longer needed an air tank. Yet he was still far too weak to walk, and so still required the wheelchair. It grated on him, and he had more than once accused James of not caring enough to do his job. It was one of many reoccurring explosive arguments.

"Have you fed the dog?" Elliot asked.

"Not yet, today," James said, handing Elliot a shot glass of his medication. Elliot knocked it back, swallowing hard and making a face.

"See that you do," he said, sounding a little strained as he handed the glass back to James. "Since we will not be back until tomorrow afternoon."

"As you wish," James said. He stood behind Elliot's wheelchair and together, they gazed at each other's reflections in the mirror. James reached out, his sleeve brushing over Elliot's porcelain cheek as his hand traveled down. Elliot felt as well as witnessed the wine red blood creep up his neck and flood his face. James smiled, touching the cameo stickpin, adjusting it ever so slightly.

"There," James said. "Perfect."

"It was already perfect," Elliot grumbled under his breath.

"No," James said condescendingly. "But I fixed it."

Scratching at the bedroom door, and the sound of a small bell. James rested his hand on Elliot's shoulder, squeezing it as he turned his head to glance behind him.

"Should I let him in?" the demon doctor asked idly.

"If you must," Elliot said, clearing his throat, his head still swimming from the blush. "I did tell you to feed him, anyway."

"Right." James started for the door, crossing the room in four long strides. Elliot waited patiently as he heard soft padding follow James' footsteps back. He lowered his hand, finally feeling a nuzzle against his fingers. He looked down and allowed a half smile to touch his lips, running his hand though Clarence Dosett's long, tangled hair.

His elder brother looked up at him with the eyes of a subdued animal, large and fearful, yet complacent. He patted Clarence's neck and felt the thick leather collar that was resting there, the attached bell jingling dolefully.

Clarence hadn't spoken much in the past thirteen years. His primary method of communication had been grunts, whimpers, and occasionally a begging nudge.

Some of it was due to conditioning. He had spent his time being forced to wander naked through the house on all fours, ignored by the servants and treated like a pet by his new masters. He had to eat off the floor, drink out of a bowl, and no one ever addressed him by his name. It was always "dog" or "pet".

Most of it, however, was due to the fact that James had eaten his tongue.

James snapped his fingers, whistling sharply. "Come on. Let's go downstairs and feed you."

Clarence turned around, going to the demon's side obediently. James smiled, pulling a small tennis ball out of his pocket and holding it aloft.

"Good boy," he cooed. Clarence's eyes brightened, and James dangled the ball in front of him for a moment before letting it drop. Clarence pounced on the ball, nuzzling it with his nose so that it rolled out of the bedroom and into the hall. He chased it all the way down the stairs.

James smirked and followed him out, closing the door as he exited.

The thing about Heaven was that even its CEO was always on vacation, which made it nearly impossible to ever get ahold of him. Satan never understood where the guy came across all of the energy to do absolutely nothing. It was almost like on the seventh day of rest, God put down his gardening tools and exclaimed "Well, *that* took a lot of me. Time for a martini." And then just never picked them back up again. No wonder the entire world had gone to shit.

Somewhere, in the archives of some old medieval church forgotten to time, Satan's fall could be traced back to a single sentence. "Frankly, I think we need a new face for the company; you're starting to make us look bad."

Satan had just stepped back onto the property for the first time in a thousand-and-some-odd years. He was existing proof that there wasn't much to say for formal restraining orders, especially when Heaven's strict anti-violence policy kept them from being reinforced. The worst he received were several nasty glares as he sauntered through the pearly gates. He just smiled and waved.

In truth, he always avoided Heaven at all costs and would rather slice off a toe than go back. But an unannounced intrusion was the only way for anyone from Hell to get an audience with 'the big man upstairs' (a ridiculous epithet, as there was nothing 'big' about him – God was only 5'7"). Besides, Satan knew that things has a better chance of getting accomplished if he just did them from the get-go.

Now he found himself standing beside a sparkling blue pool the size of a football field. Michael, the world's oldest brown-noser, was out in the middle doing laps while God was lounging in a chair not far away, working on his tan.

Satan stood there and waited to see how long it would take for De'ot the "all-knowing" to notice he had arrived.

"I'm going to call security," God said, with the air of someone who already felt like security was on its way.

"All right," Satan said, looming over the chair and making a point of casting as long a shadow as possible. "Mind looking over these papers, while we wait?"

God looked up and furrowed his brow, sliding his sunglasses down his nose.

"What do you want?" he snapped.

Satan shook the heavy folder in his hand.

God sighed irately, setting his tanning foil down and sliding his sunglasses up into his perfectly combed hair.

"If I look at it, will you go away?" The Almighty was already sliding the folder from Satan's hands, noting how much heavier it was than it looked.

"I think you made a mistake," Satan said.

"I *never* make mistakes." God was more than a little insulted, flipping through the paperwork in such a way that he couldn't have been processing the information. "How am I *supposedly* mistaken?"

Satan rolled his eyes and took back the folder, flipping up a few pages and flashing a neatly typed profile with a singular picture. "You know him?"

God narrowed his eyes. "Meriwether Hayward. I know him."

"He prefers 'Lady', I hear."

"Right," God said dismissively. "He Fell a long time ago. They did all the paperwork. *You* guys processed it."

"Except we didn't, because you didn't file the paperwork properly. There is no reason stated for *why* he Fell."

"Isn't this a job better left to the boys in our processing centers?" God picked up his foil again.

"I'd actually like to see it solved before the End Times." Satan tapped the paper. "What did he do? We can solve this in a few pen strokes."

"It was terrible and offensive enough to get him damned. What more do you people need?"

"You know, unlike some, our company policy prevents us from unjust persecution..."

"Well, well. Look at what Hell coughed up." Michael emerged from the pool, grabbing a white towel to rub over his blonde curls. "Come back for your old job?"

"Thanks," Satan said dryly, "but I hear he likes the way you jerk him off just fine."

"You got big." Michael slammed a flat hand against Satan's stomach. "I'm thinking of letting myself go as well. Coasting into retirement with a protective layer on these flattened abs."

God slid his sunglasses back down over his eyes and leaned back in his chair, perfectly content to let them duke it out over his head.

"I'm not done with you," Satan said, pointing an accusing finger at God, quickly reaching the end of his patience.

"I think you are," Michael said dangerously. "Any further grievances you have, you can send in through Processing. This is their department, the Almighty has more important things to do."

Satan's eyes narrowed, and he glowered down at God again.

"You are going to get *moles*," he said through his teeth. "And skin cancer."

"Are you finished?" God snapped. Satan growled. Shoving his folder under his armpit, he clenched his fists, his arms rigid at his sides as he stalked away, back towards the pearly gates.

Fuck this place.

Fuck its impractical gold streets. Fuck its 24/7 blinding sunlight. Fuck its sanitized surface that beautifully masked the filthy, squirming heap of grubs and maggots that angels and God actually *were*.

He would force them to correct this error. He wasn't going to let this go.

Satan never was one for just letting things go.

CHAPTER 9

It had rained earlier that evening. The cobblestone streets were slick. The soles of Lawrence's inexpensive shoes slipped and skid as he ran, jamming his toes into rough, raised edges. He winced but recollected himself each time, desperation propelling him down pitch-black avenues. The gas lamps that lined the streets died as soon as he approached them, snuffed out quietly like candles. He had no idea why, but that was not his most immediate concern.

How long had the man been following him? Had it been as soon as he left dinner with Lord and Lady Clifton?

And how long had there been *two* of them?

Lawrence was running out of open streets. He was coming to a small bridge, across which was nothing but a stretch of slums – more than likely where these brigands had sprang from. He did not want to dash directly into their territory, where it would be easier for them to rob him and God only knew what else. He had no choice but to veer into an alley. It was either that or backtrack. He had passed his house several blocks back, but he did not want them to know where he lived.

If he could shake them long enough to circle back, he could slip in through his side door. If he could even get *that* close, he would feel much better screaming for the constabulary.

Another gas lamp sputtered and died.

The alley was crawling with vermin and stray cats. It smelled like garbage and piss, and he had to pick his way past piles of unknown composition – which considerably slowed his progress. He glanced behind him, a short tress of oily ginger hair falling into his wide, panicked eyes.

He could not see either of the men behind him. And he could no longer hear footsteps. Lawrence paused to take a deep breath, placing his palms against a slimy brick wall and sighing, closing his eyes. They had stopped following him after all.

The blow that pushed him up against the wall was crushing. His ribs crunched inward, threatening to puncture his heaving lungs. Pain shot up from the base of his spine to his skull, making large grey spots appear when he opened his eyes. He could barely breathe, and the arm pressed against his back kept him effectively pinned to the wall.

"Squirmy." The voice that spoke was genteel and bookish, if not unnecessarily dry.

"They get like that after a few blocks." The one that kept him pinioned had a deeper voice, a jungle cat. "Scalpel."

Lawrence's body jerked as the back of his dinner jacket was ripped open. His shirt came next, and he could not even fathom what sort of preternatural creature could pull apart wool like that with only one hand.

A pause, followed by a pinch, and then burning. Lawrence whimpered and tried to move, but it was useless. The man closest to him made an impatient sound. Lawrence felt cold fingers wrap around the back of his head and pull it back, briefly, before smashing it against the brick.

His body went numb, and he was gone.

Henry swore under his breath and continued to drag the scalpel down the length of the man's pale, freckled back – following the slight curve of the spine.

"A competitor?" James asked conversationally.

"He tried to be." Henry handed the medical tool back, switching off which hand was holding up the body as he rolled up his sleeves. "Violet got him to sell."

"A very convincing woman, your Violet." James watched as Henry gripped the limp man's neck, shoving his hand into the deep incision. Flesh peeled apart audibly, warping grotesquely as e wrapped his fingers around the spine. Henry pushed down on the neck while jerking back the spine, and there was a resounding snap. Another tug, another crack, and the spine came free completely. He tossed it to the side, hunks of meat and frayed nerves still attached, and he easy found the pocket of flesh behind the heart containing the soul. Henry put is face close to the corpse, the heat of blood and stench of organs hitting his face as he slid his tongue over the fleshy bubble, pricking it with his teeth. He pressed his lips to its firm surface, sucking the soul out through the hole his teeth created. He moaned, grinding the balls between his molars and feeling the juices gush down his throat. He had to force himself to stop, drawing back and letting the rest pour out into his hands. He looked back and flashed a grin at James, his teeth as red as his face. The soul that filled his cupped hands was bright and ruby red.

When the pocket was empty, he turned to James, offering up the soul that was in his hands. James gave him a long look before stooping, grabbing Henry's hands in his own, and dragging them up to his face, gorging on his portion of the soul – licking the remnants from Henry's gory palms.

James scrunched up his nose, wiping his mouth with the back of his hand.

"It tastes a bit like raspberry licorice," he said.

"I like it." Henry raked his hands through his hair to get it out of his face – leaving grisly streaks in the blonde.

"I can't tell if I do or not." James licked the corners of his mouth, trying to gather up the last of the taste and make up his mind.

Henry shrugged. "You don't have to eat the red ones," he said, sounding a mother compromising with her child over dinner. "I think we have reached the point in our quotas where we can both afford to be picky if we wished."

James sniffed, adjusting his glasses. "It evens out. You don't like the orange ones, do you?"

"Bloody fucking hate them."

"They taste like citrus," James said, turning to leave the alleyway.

"Taste like piss, is what," Henry muttered, following the other demon out.

"I hope you do not encourage this form of pickiness in your children," James said, slowing his pace enough so that Henry could catch up and they could walk side-by-side.

"Not usually," Henry said, fiddling with the buttons on his coat. There was one in particular that he always played with because it was hanging loose. He wanted to see how many times he could pull on it before the thread snapped. "I mean, I don't *care*. Violet is the one who undermines me. She enforces all of the rules – bedtime by eight, eat every vegetable on your plate or you get no dessert. That sort of thing. I don't really understand – I mean, are they considered too young to have opinions? Do grown humans only eat vegetables because it was instilled in them as children that broccoli is a gateway to pastries? Would they live on an empire built of cake and run around interrupting each other and whooping like savages if, as children, they were allowed to choose their own meals and not be stashed away in closets by eight o' clock at night?"

"Do you really stash them in closets?" James gave him a curious look.

Henry shrugged. "I don't know. The nursemaid whisks them away and I can only assume. They're always in bed when I go kiss them goodnight but who knows what occurs after that? Their beds are always mysteriously pristine in the morning, so you have to wonder."

James grinned. "You kiss your children goodnight?"

"You would too," Henry said defensively, turning down the street that would eventually lead to his house. "The oldest, though, he doesn't like to be kissed anymore. It's very disheartening."

"Do you ever think about their souls?"

Henry stopped in his tracks, looking truly affronted. James glanced at him and lifted an eyebrow.

"What?" the demon doctor asked.

"You mean do I ever think about *eating* them?" Henry sounded scandalized.

"Why not?" James asked.

Henry paused to think about it. He opened his mouth to say something and then closed it again, furrowing his brow and rolling his lips inward.

"Hm," he said. "Well, I don't know."

"They are probably too sweet," James offered by way of possible explanation.

"Probably." Henry nodded thoughtfully. "I suppose, though, that I *have* thought about it. They are all small and fluttery and it would be *easy*. Sometimes, when they cough too hard, I think about how one more robust hack would have them spitting up their souls into their hand. I know the colors. Just like everyone else, you can see it in their eyes. Those thin rings around the irises... and all of them different colors. It's hard to tell with Nellie – she's the smallest, but Edward's is fully developed. His soul is blue." Henry smiled, running his tongue over his lips. James shivered as well and they shared a knowing look. Blue was the richest, best color to taste.

"How about the others?" James asked, he could already feel his stomach gurgling like he had not eaten in days.

"Claire is orange," Henry said, going down the line. "Emmet is green. Ettie is white. And as I said, I don't know Nellie's yet."

"And what color is Violet's soul?" James asked, lowering his voice.

"Silver," Henry didn't even have to think about it. He had spent unhealthy amounts of time over thirteen years gazing into her eyes, memorizing those perfect slim, silver rings that circumscribed her leaf brown irises like wires.

"Elliot's soul is black as pitch," James said a little smugly, thinking about those bitter dark circles – rings of tar around cold, unyielding metal.

"I can only imagine," Henry's voice sounded strained with need at the thought, "how that might taste."

For a minute they stood there, the poison acids of their insides roiling. Each were able to picture, if only for a moment, how the two souls might taste *together*. Silver wire and black tar – oily, metallic, and perhaps a little like licorice.

"Perhaps..." Henry said thoughtfully.

"Perhaps," James echoed back.

Neither really said any more than that. It wasn't necessary... they were thinking the same thing.

"You have not been to bed."

From the corner of his eye, Elliot saw the demon collapse into an armchair. James slumped into the plush seat, his black curls bunching up as he slid.

"I have not," Elliot replied at last, folding a few more documents and making a nice, crisp crease with his pale fingertip. "You were out late."

"We had to chase the guy." James huffed. "Several blocks."

"You are out of shape." Elliot dipped his pen back into its inkwell. James pursed his lips and sat up straight, indignant at the implication.

"Next time," the demon said dryly, "I will let *you* chase him."

The look Elliot gave him was long, withering, and not at all forgiving.

James sighed. "I didn't mean it."

"This isn't my fault. I have held up my end." Elliot tightened his grip on his pen. "You won't hold up yours."

"I have *been* holding up my end. These things take time." James stood, making his way over to the desk. He set his hand down gently on top of the documents, meeting Elliot's eyes. Elliot held his gaze for a long minute before yanking the pen from its inkwell and jabbing it temperamentally into the back of James' hand.

James did not flinch. He continued to hold the eye contact. Elliot set his teeth on edge, wrenching the pen, digging it as deep as he possibly could.

"Are you finished?" the demon asked quietly. Without waiting for a reply, he lifted his hand and forced the pen from Elliot's fingers. Grasping it in his own hand, he yanked it out and let it clatter to the desk.

Black blood oozed sluggishly from the wound, which already smelled like it was rotting. Elliot looked away, his posture still rigid.

"I did not," Elliot said, "give you my father's soul so you could continue to be a poor excuse for a demon."

"No," James said tersely. "You gave me your father's soul because you wanted to watch him die. And I let you. And you *liked it.*"

"I have seen many die since then," Elliot reminded him.

"And you will see many more go, still." James' hand was already beginning to heal. He cradled it now, fingering the hole gingerly. "You are in an ill mood. More so than usual."

"As you pointed out," Elliot said. "I have not been to bed." He set his hands on the arms of his wheelchair. "You can take me there now. I am through here."

"Of course." James moved behind him, grasping the handles and backing the wheelchair away from the desk, turning it around to face the door before progressing. "Do you require anything more than usual tonight? Perhaps some laudanum to help you sleep?"

"You have grown very fond of medicating me," Elliot noted.

"I have only your best interests at heart," James assured him.

"Mm." Elliot's hands tightened on the arms of his wheelchair. "I wonder."

CHAPTER 10

He was a quarter of an hour late. Hell had a highway but it was only four lanes and it always seemed to be rush hour. Not to mention it was nearly impossible to go any faster than 60mph at any given time (it was a well-known fact that anyone driving ten miles under the speed limit in life ended up doing time in purgatory out of principle).

Now he stood on the doorstep of the stern apartment building, rain soaking the shoulders of his thin coat and rolling off the brim of his squat bowler hat. Francis Hislop sighed and hit the buzzer that was connected to his boss' apartment unit, hoping for a prompt response.

Ten minutes passed before the door opened and Lady appeared in the entrance. Francis barely recognized the Unchaste who, judging from the extra pudge on his belly, had undoubtedly named gluttony his favorite sin.

"Don't you dare say anything," Lady said before Francis could even open his mouth.

"I wasn't going to!" the intern said defensively, clutching his wet arms. "Can I come in, please? It's devilishly cold."

Lady narrowed his eyes. "I suppose." He stepped aside, allowing enough room for Francis to enter before shutting the door. "I'm up this way." He waved towards the staircase. "You're late, you know." Lady started up the stairs, mincing prim little steps.

"I know," Francis said, not even bothering to explain the highway situation as they made their quick ascent up creaky wooden boards. "How are things going for you, here?"

"Very well, as you can see." Lady unlocked a little narrow crème-colored door, stepping into a cozy apartment done tastefully in powder blue and white. Fashionable colors, if not drab enough to suit him. It must have come prepared that way. "There are *so many* eyes, Frank. You would not believe."

"Wouldn't I?" Francis bit his tongue too late as the comment slithered out. "I'm glad you can enjoy them – someone has to, right? I always preferred hearts, personally…" He looked around, trying to avoid meeting Lady's unforgiving glare. "…Well. This place is *very* spacious."

"Stop talking, Frank." Lady walked over to a small tea cart where a pot of steaming coffee and an arrangement of cups had been set out. "Have a seat. Coffee?"

"Yes, thank you," Francis replied, thankful to be back on familiar ground as he took his seat gingerly on a brocade couch. "So, why did you ask me to come out here? I finally got around to checking the answering machine but none of your messages were very specific."

"There is a good reason for that." Lady handed over a soft pink flower-shaped cup, filled to the brim with coffee that smelled strongly of a dark, rich roast. "Hell is filled with liars, thieves, and lawyers and I don't trust anyone not to go poking around where they aren't wanted."

Francis nodded, feeling his own sense of apprehension mounting. This was not a very promising build-up. "What exactly have we done wrong?"

Lady scowled, his cup paused halfway to his mouth. "What makes you ask that? *We* have done nothing wrong. *You* are the one leaving the phone calls unanswered."

"Well yes, but I…"

"Not that I'm blaming you of course. If you answered the phones all day you would never get anything else done. I am simply pointing out that if someone *were* to call about a possible oversight in one or several of the files I could not be blamed, because the error would be in how they were processed…"

"Just one minute!" Francis set his cup down indignantly. "What are you trying to pin on me?"

"Nothing." Lady blinked innocently. "Do I sound like I am trying to accuse you of anything?"

"What is this 'oversight'…"

"*Theoretical* oversight."

"…Right. And does it have anything to do with why Satan called the other day?"

Lady spit out his coffee back into his cup, coughing up what few drops he had swallowed into an embroidered handkerchief.

"I'm sorry. You said Satan…?"

"He left three different messages," Francis said, and added with a hint of pride, "I didn't listen to any of them."

"What the hell!" Lady set his cup down and his head sank despairingly into his gloved hands. "Frank! You don't just *ignore Satan!*"

"But our policy is to ignore everyone," Francis argued.

"Not the CEO of Hell! The *Eternal Destroyer!*"

"Well he isn't on our 'call back' list so excuse me for living."

Lady took a deep breath, trying to collect himself and his thoughts. "How long ago did he call?"

"A few weeks," Francis said.

"All right." Lady felt he knot in his intestines easing, but only slightly. "Well, if he hasn't cast either of us into eternal flames then I suppose it couldn't have been *that* important."

"Maybe a routine employee survey?" Francis offered weakly.

Lady nodded. "We're going with that." He stared dismally at his coffee cup. "Anything *else* important you would like to inform me about, while you're at it?"

"That's about all I've got," Francis responded. "Processing continues to call. The paperwork has been piling on your desk. Quite a few FINAL NOTICES, etc."

Lady waved a hand dismissively. "Anything else?"

"No. That's about it."

"I appreciate you holding things down in my absence," Lady said. "I will write you a stunning recommendation at the end of your internship."

Francis smiled brightly. "Thank you, sir. It is very much appreciated."

"How many years do you have left?"

"Forty-three. The century is flying by."

"Tell me about it. In about that amount of time I'd like to have this affair wrapped up and move on to the next one. Henry and James are going to need a little bit of guidance switching directions because…well, you know how demons can be. They get settled into a rut and they become comfortable, and then they never want to expand their horizons. But there are far better souls out there than that of a bitter widow and an overly-ambitious boy completely lacking in vision."

"Harsh, boss." Francis helped himself to a refill of his coffee, this time stirring in a spoonful of sugar as the two of them lapsed into silence, each mulling over the situation at present.

"I hope they assign me another intern as lazy as you," Lady said after a while. "I don't know what I would do with an earnest worker."

"I was earnest!" Francis set his spoon down across the edge of his saucer. "Once upon a time."

"I set you straight. It was more work than it should have been. But laziness is a skill you can carry with you for the rest of your career, so cherish the things I have taught you. Or neglected to teach you, rather."

"Ignorance is bliss," Francis said, with no uncertain amount of irony.

There was something about his sister, though Edward had no clue what it was. Nellie never did anything special. She was a baby for Christ's sake, and babies were never known for being particularly enthralling. She did drool excessively, which he found mildly disgusting. Other than that, she was a pasty ball of smiles and lace the size of a Christmas turkey.

Yet there was *something* he couldn't shake.

He had caught himself staring at her across the lawn more often than once, while she played with her nurse and he lazily batted a tennis ball around with his other sister, Claire. Sometimes he would gaze at her all throughout dinner, his own food left to go cold and untouched. Sometimes she noticed and would laugh. Other times she ignored him completely. It never made a difference. All he could think about was how sweet she smelled – like wild blueberries or sugary plums. The scent alone could make his head spin, and he had to refrain from spending hours in her nursery with his nose buried in one of her fresh napkins. He gnawed on the corners and huffed that smell and dreamed of warm amber beads, bursting between his teeth – the shells slippery and gritty against his molars.

He didn't know where that particular imagery had come from, nor did he have a name for it. All he could say for sure was that ever since his horns had started coming in, his stomach growled every time he was around his sister. And he had vicious nightmares… every one of them involving breaking open her tiny chest and ripping out her organs to get to *something* inside.

Claire did not have her horns yet, and that was probably why she didn't understand. Her scent was not as tantalizing. She brought to mind tropical sunsets and fresh round oranges, like the kind their father had imported and sliced to accompany poached eggs in the morning. When Edward was around her, his head did not start spinning, and he never had dreams of ripping her apart and digging through her internal organs.

That was probably how they managed to continue getting along so well.

She enjoyed needlepoint, the dullest of all feminine occupations. She was engaged in some at that very moment as they sat in the shade of a poplar tree, partially concealed by its generous branches.

"You're thinking about something," she said without looking up, pulling her needle through a taut space of silk and leaving behind another crimson stitch.

"Generally," he said, bored. He was stretched out across the grass with his head resting in her lap, observing her work from a position underneath the embroidery hoop. It was at least somewhat interesting to see her quick fingers flashing, her needle vanishing as soon as it appeared.

"Anything of merit?" she asked, in a way that suggested he was only capable of trivial thought.

"I was thinking about cannibalism," he said.

"How disturbing."

"Well, no." He raked a hand through his messy brown hair, feeling the dull tips of his horns – barely concealed. "I just keep wondering... why is it illegal?"

She tied off her stitch, snapping the floss and switching it out for another color. "Because it is morally reprehensible."

"But why?" he badgered.

"I'm not sure," she said. "It must be somewhere in the Bible."

He nodded solemnly. "I hadn't thought of that." In truth, he had. "Yet did Jesus not bid us to partake of his body and his blood? And do we not continue this very ritual during Communion?"

"It isn't cannibalism if Jesus is in the equation," Claire said. "He is divine. And cannibalism is the consumption of *human* flesh."

Edward pouted. "Well... he was human at the last supper!"

"Jesus was never human, he only inhabited human form. Daddy explained this, remember? He said spirits often take human form but that doesn't make them any *less* spirit."

"Oh, yeah." Edward sighed. "Because you asked about how the nephilim differed from angels. And he said..."

"And he explained the difference between a divine creature conceiving a child with a human, and a spirit taking on a corporeal form."

"Wait!" Edward exclaimed excitedly. "Wasn't Jesus something like a nephilim?"

"No. Don't be stupid."

"He was born of an angel and a human...?"

"He was born of..." Claire paused. "*God* and a human. But ... Mary was a virgin..." She paused, setting aside her needlework to look down at him, her brow furrowing. "Oh... bugger it all. You can't be a virgin and have a baby, can you? I think mama said that once."

"I think she said that *in* church," Edward noted victoriously.

"So Jesus was truly flesh? I guess that means…" She shook her head and scoffed. "Well whatever it *does* mean, it does *not* mean cannibalism is encouraged! And especially not when it involves your baby sister. So drop it." She went back to her needlework.

"I wasn't actually going to eat her!" Edward whined. "But if you think about it, no one would miss her. I mean mother might and father would but… only for a little while. And they can always have another baby."

"What parts of her would you eat?" Claire asked, her morbid curiosity getting the better of her.

"All of the inside parts," Edward said enthusiastically. "Think about it! Human blood pudding and kidney pie and liver sausage." He didn't mention the amber beads; the things he *knew* were inside but could not prove. "Does none of that sound the least bit interesting to you?"

"I think I'd like to try the meat," Claire said after a moment's thought. "I wonder what a human steak would taste like, done tender and rare and served with a nice glass of wine."

"You've never had wine," Edward pointed out.

"If I'm going to eat a human, I don't see what's going to stop me from drinking wine," Claire said.

Edward sat up, narrowly avoiding knocking his head against her hoop. She moved it out of the way regardless, casting an annoyed look his way.

"Do you think," he wondered aloud, "that if I did eat someone, Jesus would forgive me?"

Claire regarded him with very solemn dark eyes, the same color as their mother's.

"I don't see why he shouldn't," she said. "If you were sorry."

"What if I wasn't sorry?" he asked.

"Then why would it matter if he forgives you?"

"I want to go to Heaven," Edward said.

Claire's eyes sparkled. "Daddy says that none of us are."

She laughed, and she sounded far too much like Henry.

CHAPTER 11

Elliot peeled back the pages of the crisp documents one by one, his fingertip sliding down every line as he scrutinized the terms of the contract. He read everything thoroughly before signing, always, even if he knew the contract holder would be dead before the evening was out.

It was just a good habit to develop.

His guest was drowning in his own sweat. The man could produce water as well as any juiced melon. Elliot was trying not to think about it, about how the man's very elbows were sweating and seeping through the fine linen of the expensive tablecloth. He knew James noticed as well and was bothered, but that would not stop the demon from splitting open their greasy guest like a butchered pig to get to the soul within. Which, Elliot had been informed, was a very delectable shade of purple. He never bothered to ask how James knew these things.

"All seems to be in order, Mr. Bornholdt," Elliot said, looking up briefly as he whipped out his expensive, sleek fountain pen. His guest swallowed hard and fought to clear his nervous expression with a smile, fidgeting with his cravat as the gleaming tip of Elliot's pen scratched across the surface of the paper – leaving behind curling trails of an elegant signature.

"Thank you, Mr. Dosett," the guest said, his voice cracking a little. "It has been a pleasure doing business with you, as always."

"As always." Elliot flashed him the barest half-smile as he slid the papers away and dropped his pen back into its inkwell. "Will you dine with us this evening?"

'Us'. How strange, the guest thought, that he should refer to himself as well as his doctor – who stood behind the wheelchair as stiffly as a servant, yet stared over the nobleman's shoulder as attentively as a business partner.

He did not give himself time to dwell on it. The less speculated, the better.

"I would be honored!" the guest replied belatedly, his jittery smile still plastered across his face as his eyes flickered from doctor to lord, uncertain of where to settle. "If ah – I may be permitted to refresh myself before then?"

"Of course." Elliot placed his fingertips together. "A servant will see you are accommodated."

The guest stood and bowed before turning to leave, forgetting the papers entirely and leaving them on the table in front of Elliot. The grave noble waited for the door to close before slumping in his wheelchair and passing his hand over his eyes.

"Eat him quickly," Elliot muttered. "I don't know if I can make it through dinner."

"I think you will be fine," James said off-handedly. "He wonders about you."

"What about me?"

"About us, I should say." The demon smirked, as if the thought greatly amused him.

Elliot sighed. "Another burden of the trade."

"Hardly," James corrected him, setting a small wooden case on the table – opening it up to reveal Elliot's medicine. With practice eased, he readied the evening's dose. "It is more a burden of your refusal to find a wife."

"I have no need of a wife," Elliot said, cutting a glare quickly at James. "Or children."

"Intend to live forever, do you?" James drew the medication up through the needle.

Elliot's gaze was long and severe. "I thought that was the plan."

"It would be difficult to collect your soul if you never gave it up." James carefully unbuttoned the lord's cuffs, rolling up his sleeve. "No matter how clever you are, the devil always get his due."

Elliot did not approve of the direction this conversation was spiraling towards.

"Is that not a touch cliché?" the lord asked, disgruntled.

James shrugged, and his needle pricked Elliot's thin skin, met with almost no resistance.

"I expect that sort of thing from Henry. Not you." Elliot sucked in a breath through his teeth at the sting. "And even if I were to *consider* getting married, I do not have the time to court anyone properly. As far as I understand, marriages are very different from business transactions. I can't just sign my name on a printed line for a woman and let you devour her father an hour later."

James laughed, withdrawing the needle. "Why not?"

"It's so uncouth."

"And since when does that bother you?"

Elliot yanked his sleeve back down. "We are not discussing it further."

"What are you afraid of?" James asked. "That she will interrupt some precious aspect of your routine?" The demon doctor adjusted his glasses, tilting his head so that the dim lamplight reflected off the lenses. "I hate to be the one to inform you that you are among the dullest of society's lords. Everyone knows your name and cowers at its utterance yet are unaware that they shy away from the equivalent of a hissing cat, who is wasting his youth behind velvet draperies and buried under documents. You know…" The demon leaned forward, his final verbal blow at the ready. "You are turning into your father."

Elliot slammed his fist down on the arm of his wheelchair. "I am *not!*"

"Oh you are!" James cackled, his breathy laughter bringing a pink flush to his cheeks. "Young Lord Hiram Dosett. Society's most elegant grouch."

Elliot's lip curled. "You are about to be society's most homeless demon."

"Go ahead." James was still giggling, bracing himself against a chair before falling into it, covering his face. "Throw me out. Have fun operating that lovely little elevator on your own on your way to bed."

Cold coffee splashed against his cheek. James pursed his lips and sat up straight, bringing up the edge of his white doctor's coat to wipe it away indignantly, checking for spots on his glasses.

"That was unnecessary," the demon said, clearing his throat.

"What the hell is wrong with you?" Elliot demanded.

"It was amusing, that's all. You are so against becoming the man who founded the empire you conquered." James shrugged. "Just because you killed him doesn't mean you can't admire him."

"I see nothing to admire in the man who had every intention of sending me away to a hospital where I'd be strapped down and drugged for the rest of my life," Elliot snarled. "You share a problem with everyone else. You can't see the man I knew. You see steel beams and ships and unshakeable buildings, and all I remember is the look he gave me after my first prognosis. He knew I was going to die, and he couldn't wait."

"There are facets of human interaction I will never understand," James said. "One of such being the complexities of the relationship between a father and son."

He whisked the medical case away from the table after putting everything back in its place. A long silence fell.

"Do you wish to refresh yourself, as well?" James asked.

"No," Elliot replied.

"Drucilla Kerslake is eligible, I hear," the demon suggested innocently. "Her father is Lord Blair Kerslake."

Elliot massaged his temples. Clearly he was not going to hear the end of this soon. "I thought Blair Kerslake had a public disgrace not too long ago."

"He did." James nodded. "You can imagine how thrilled he would be to marry off his remaining child to a man of your wealth and influence. All the easier to ingratiate himself back into royal favor."

Elliot scoffed. "I have no wish to be a stepping stone for another man. Nor do I wish to attach a sullied family name to my own."

"For someone who declared only minutes ago that he had no need for a wife, you are being very particular," James rebuked.

"Drucilla Kerslake is as undesirable as she is attainable."

"Ah, the truth comes out!" James grinned. "So the woman is corpulent. I never would have thought a word such as that would intimidate a man like you."

"I am not intimidated!" Elliot protested indignantly.

James clucked his tongue. "I am very disappointed."

"I am not...!" Elliot set his teeth on edge. He tried to grab his wheels and push himself back, away from the table, but James' foot wedged against the back of the chair stopped him.

"Do not act a child," James said reproachfully. "Drucilla is a wife easily attained and just as easily ignored. It would be good for you. As your doctor I prescribe marriage as the next step in your healing process."

"You are ridiculous." Elliot gave in to sulking. "I don't even know how to begin courting – or how to start a prospective marriage correspondence."

"I had assumed as much. Which is why I have already arranged a meeting."

"You…!" Elliot pinched the bridge of his nose and took a deep breath. "As long as you didn't invite her to dinner."

"No, I would never. Especially when you refuse to refresh yourself."

"I sometimes think you exist solely to make my life more difficult."

A taciturn smile touched James' lips. "I do not know what would ever give you that impression."

Greed was six feet tall and all leg, so smooth and shiny that she appeared more metal than flesh even when doing her best to look human. Everything from her sleek black ponytail to her straight, slim pencil skirt looked like it had been slicked down with oil. Even her eyes, the color of worn dollar bills – currency passed through too many greasy hands. And of all the Sins, she was Satan's least favorite to work with.

She sat in the chair across from his desk, and he couldn't help but wonder if she would leave behind a stain.

She was one of the best, if not *the* best in her field. She usually handled the big cases – corporations that glutted themselves until they toppled and declared bankruptcy, mob bosses in charge of powerful drug rings that ran entire cities. She liked order and she liked efficiency, operating methodically like a new machine with no kinks whatsoever in her gears. He knew she would be perfect for what he wanted done, he just wasn't sure how he was going to convince her to do it. How did one bribe a woman who already had her claws in a piece of everything?

A slim white cigarette settled between her thick berry red lips. The tip began to glow bright orange without any provocation from a light. She regarded him over the rims of small rectangular sunglasses perched on the tip of her sharp nose and a stream of smoke escaped her luscious mouth.

"You look a little grim this evening," she said. "Is this about my quarterly reports?"

"No, nothing like that," Satan said, his fingers itching to reach for his own menthols. So far he was managing to resist the urge. "It appears one of our Unchaste has dropped off the map."

"How do you lose one of your own Fallen angels?"

"Well, he isn't properly documented, for one thing," Satan said. "And he is impossible to get in touch with. The only way seems to be his office phone and I have a sneaking suspicion it has been unplugged. That and he disappeared into mortal earth a while back and no one has heard from him since. Every now and then reports might slide across a desk but they always come through his intern who is equally impossible to contact. My point is, I know you have some people down in the fourth circle who can help."

"For a price." Greed nodded, holding her cigarette out and examining the burning tip with feigned interest. "There is a hefty price tag attached to every exclusive service."

The fourth circle was already one of Hell's most over-funded layers. Satan wasn't going to sweat the details, however.

"Of course," he said. "Whatever you need, I will supply it just to get this sorted out. Frankly, it's giving me a headache having to run round in circles with Heaven and still get nowhere."

"Well," Greed snorted. "That's Heaven, for you. I need to know more about this Unchaste. How did he Fall? What are his vices?"

"I have no clue," Satan replied dryly. "It had to be something absolutely vile, God refuses to speak of it at all. That is partially why I am so interested in recovering him. If I have a formidable weapon on my hands, I want to utilize it."

"I need records," Greed said. "I can't pursue a name and a profession. I need the dirty details. You send me in there with nothing and that's exactly what you're going to get in return."

Satan rubbed his face. Of course – why had he ever expected this might get easier?

"I know of only one person who might have the slightest clue." And that required another trip all the way up to Heaven. What a joyous prospect.

Greed tapped the end of her cigarette over Satan's ash tray, shrugging and returning the wet, red-rimmed end to her lips.

"You should probably get in touch with him," she said. "I cannot make any progress without information."

"Wonderful," Satan said sarcastically, pulling out an unopened pack of menthols and slamming them against his wide palm. "Just fucking wonderful."

Drucilla Kerslake had maroon colored eyes. Which, James understood, was an oddity amongst humans. She was also paler than Elliot, a trait which he understood to be even rarer. Yet where Elliot's coloration left some hope that he might one day darken should he ever venture out into the sunlight, her skin gave no such illusions, being so entirely white that it could very well have been reflective if her crème colored parasol were not sheltering her from the horrors of the afternoon rays. Her eyelashes, eyebrows, and thick wavy hair were all the same pure color; threads as translucent as spiderwebs pulled up into a fashionably large style and bolstered by multiple hair pieces.

James hoped she had not been allowed to dress herself that morning, because the black and tan tartan dress she wore flattered exactly no part of her.

Both of her feet touched the ground and the carriage sprang up an extra inch. The gathered household servants held their breath and averted their eyes, embarrassed on Lord Elliot's behalf. Their lord could seldom be accused of bad taste, and surely never anticipated that this would be the form of his future bride. Each of them could only imagine what was running through his head in that moment.

Really, the only thing on Elliot's mind was what James could possibly be thinking.

Drucilla lifted her unoccupied hand and cupped it over her brow, shielding sensitive eyes to get a better, unhindered look at her fiancé. She was equally unimpressed by his appearance. For while all the world knew Elliot Dosett was wheelchair-bound, she had expected more from the so-deemed 'man of the age'. Not, as her father reminded her, that she was in position to be picky. She supposed she should just consider herself lucky that he was fairly young and not one of those lecherous old hawks.

"Welcome, my lady." James tried to salvage what remained of the botched air of hospitality. Silence followed his greeting, and he kicked the nearest wheel of Elliot's chair.

"We are so pleased to have you with us at last," Elliot spoke through his teeth as he forced a smile, unsure of how he was expected to act. Drucilla sensed it, gathering up some of her skirt and lifting the hem as she dipped into a curtsy, her own smile tight and thin.

"And I to be here, my lord." Her voice was husky and low. "You have a beautiful home. Your estate is … very impressive."

"It keeps out the wind," Elliot said dismissively, his sharp, unforgiving gaze falling onto the servants. "Enough, now. Return to your duties."

A collective sigh of relief rippled down the line as the servants broke apart and scattered, eager to escape the building tension. Elliot turned his head back to his guest as they fled.

"Shall we go in?" Even as he spoke, James gripped the handles of his wheelchair and was turning him back towards the door.

Drucilla followed them inside, gravel crunching underneath her stout heels. Dusky dark rose tea was waiting for them in the drawing room, as well as a plate of vanilla and walnut scones.

"I know you have just arrived," Elliot said as they took their places at the small table. "But my aunt and her husband will be joining us for dinner tonight unexpectedly. I hope that does not perturb you."

Drucilla's smile was as tight as a drum. "Not in the least." She watched the maid pour her tea, filling the up almost to the rim but leaving room for milk and sugar.

"Your father is a gracious man to grant me your hand." Elliot was now making his best effort to be polite while James fixed his tea, as no servant was allowed. "And on such unfashionably sudden notice, as I have been courting you scarcely two months."

"Well," Drucilla waved the maid away and used delicate tongs to pick a sugar cube out from its dish. "It was either this or the nunnery."

"Oh?" Elliot asked, and James smiled.

Drucilla nodded. "And the favor of God is secondary to the favor of a wealthy man."

"Are wealthy men not God?"

"Wealthy men are a constituent of God," Drucilla responded, quick to put him back in his place. "I like to think that the Almighty has more substance to his character than bank notes and steel rails."

Elliot lifted an eyebrow. "If there is a God, and if he does care about us, then I doubt he is more sympathetic than someone like me would be."

James nearly choked while swallowing his tea. Elliot magnanimously pretended not to notice.

"You might be right," Drucilla said, stirring her tea and creating a little whirlpool in the center of the cup

147

before setting her spoon down on the edge of her saucer. "But I hope for humanity's sake that you are not."

"I think God does you one better," James said to Elliot, even though no one had asked his opinion. "Where you might care very little, he does not care at all."

"There you have it, then," Elliot said. "From the mouth of a doctor. God does exist, and he thinks we're swine."

"That's why he keeps killing you all off," James added, helpfully.

Drucilla's eyes flickered between the two, a seed of what she thought was understanding already being planted in her mind. "If God really thinks in such a way, then why doesn't he destroy us all?"

"He tries," James said, "but you keep regrouping."

"You really need to work on your inclusive language," Elliot said. Drucilla might as well have not been in the room. "One would think you do not consider yourself human."

"Well," James shrugged. "I am a man of medicine."

"And I a man of wealth," Elliot said. "And together, we have no use for God."

'Or wives,' Drucilla thought to herself, but wisely held her tongue.

CHAPTER 12

Satan knocked, and a drone answered.

He wasn't sure what he had been expecting, but it was slightly more than a murky round lens and a glaring prick of red light that seemed intent on blinding him. He scowled and squinted into the camera, but all that looked back at him was his own clean-cut reflection.

"Business please," the drone garbled, its thin propellers whirring. Satan folded his arms.

"Cut the crap, Raziel," he snapped.

"Business, please," the drone repeated, and its spastic red light flickered.

"Fuck...!" Satan held up a hand to block the light from his vision. "I need to talk to you, if you can pull your head out of your ass long enough..."

"Business – please – business..." The drone continued to sputter out the same message. Satan felt the beginnings of a painful headache begin to form in his temples. Suddenly, the red light died, and a grey shutter closed over the camera lens. The propellers slowed and the drone began to sink to the ground, falling neatly into the waiting arms of an angel in the form of a soft young man with cherubic cheeks and mess of thick, dark hair that could not decide in which direction it wanted to grow.

"Sorry," Raziel said. "I'm still working out the kinks on this model." He peered at Satan through glasses as thick as a finger. "Long time, no see. It has been... what, some two thousand years?"

"You didn't have drones last time," Satan said dryly, wondering why Heaven got drones when Hell was still sending things primarily through fax.

"They're a more recent development." Raziel looked fondly down at the spindly machine in his arms. "The Almighty wants them militarized for Armageddon. But they have a thousand other uses, including answering doors so I don't have to."

"That one isn't very good at it," Satan said, sliding his hands into his pockets.

Raziel cradled the drone closer defensively. "He tries his best!" the angel protested. "He's a newer model, don't fault him his first day on the job."

"Right, right." Satan nodded. "I'd love to stay up here and talk shop with you, but I'm on a tight schedule. I need your help."

"Of course you do." Raziel turned and disappeared into the building. "Come on in, then. Pardon the mess."

Satan nodded and only took a single step forward before his foot hit something solid. He winced and looked down, but could not quite make out what it was in the darkness.

"Have you ever heard of lamps?" he asked, picking his way across the floor carefully.

"They impede my great work." Raziel sniffed, setting his drone down on a table and flickering on a single gas lamp. It struggled to fill the cluttered room with weak yellow light, which was still better than none.

"Your toys might work better if you utilized one," Satan suggested. "Just a thought."

"Shh." Raziel waved his hand as if that were unimportant. "Why are you up here? You said you needed something."

"Yes...I have lost track of one of my Unchaste."

Raziel snorted.

"I know," Satan said, annoyed. "But I am trying to get him back. That is why I came up here, to seek the help of Heaven's oldest record-keeper..."

"And currently, its most undervalued researcher," Raziel said sulkily. "I have the cure for cancer, but do you think anyone is interested in that? No, they just want weapons..."

Satan was not about to sit through this rant.

"Meriwether Hayward," Satan cut the angel off. "Does the name sound familiar?"

"Should it?" Raziel produced a large box filled with papers divided and organized by colorful plastic tabs. "So many come through here. And you *know* how bad I am with names. Or with... talking to people in general." He pulled out a blue sleeve marked "H" and began to rifle through it.

"He sometimes goes by the name 'Lady'." Satan offered as an afterthought.

Raziel gave him an annoyed look through narrowed eyes, as if that threw off the entire system, and reached back into his box, withdrawing a yellow sleeve marked "L".

"This is why I'm so disorganized," the angel said mournfully. "Because all of you twist me in twenty different directions."

Satan didn't comment. He looked around at the organized chaos of what was countless centuries' worth of discovery crammed into a single room. The angel had a particular fondness for globes, or anything vaguely circle shaped, as much as he did for anything square that could stack well or be slid into tight corners where nothing should conceivably be able to be stored. There was a name for creatures like him, but Satan couldn't quite put his finger on it...

"Meriwether L. Hayward?" Raziel's voice had a questioning lilt as he pulled out a few stapled papers.

"Does the 'L' stand for 'Lady'?" Satan asked.

"Lou," Raziel replied, skimming through the pages.

"Of course," Satan said.

"Biblical name, Banu. Well," Raziel smiled. "That explains it."

"I'm sorry?"

"Banu is 'lady' in Persian."

"...I see." Satan held out his hand and Raziel handed him the papers. He flipped immediately to the profile, where everything was laid out neatly in plain lettering.

"*Proper Name: Meriwether Lou Hayward.*" Satan muttered the information as he read to help him process. "*Biblical Name: Banu-Azra. Breed: Angel (Dominion). Classification: Unchaste.* Good, so this is an updated file."

"Of course it is." Raziel sounded insulted.

Satan continued down.

"*Identity: Agender.* The rest of this seems fairly standard. Where is the page for vices?"

"Here." Raziel turned to the next page for him and pointed to a run of paragraphs. "Vices, information on personality and..."

"And where is history?"

"I'm getting to it." Raziel huffed. "History is on the back of that page."

Satan flipped it over. "*Ah!*" he jabbed his finger against the middle of the paper. "*Reason for Fall...*" his brow creased, and as he read on, his expression darkened. "Oh for the love of...are you *fucking with me?*"

"What?" Raziel's eyes widened. He tried to lean over to read, but Satan crumpled the paper in his fist, tossing it furiously to the side.

"Of all the asinine...!" the Lord of Hell growled, the floor underneath his feet smoldering as he stormed out the door. The entire building shook when he slammed it shut. Raziel shrank back and bent over to pick up the paper, smoothing it out with his fingertips and squinting to see what was written.

'*Reason for Fall:*' it stated, '*loss of valuable property*'.

Raziel made a face, looking at the paper questionably.

That didn't make any fucking sense.

Edward's stomach hurt.

Which didn't make sense, considering he had just eaten. Henry and Violet had left that afternoon to go visit his cousin Elliot, which meant the children had been given their own supper alone and earlier in the evening than usual. The maids had done their best to corral everyone into bed in as timely a manner as possible and Edward had been left to languish sleeplessly; the remnants of early evening sunlight were still streaming through his windows, attempting to pry apart the slit between the curtains.

He didn't know how long his belly had been aching. It felt like it had been hours. He thought about sneaking down to the kitchen and pinching something light – a pastry, maybe – but the idea of real food made him nauseous. The only thing managing to take the edge off his hunger pains was the smell of the clean linen napkin taken from a pile in his baby sister's room. Edward pressed it against his face, breathing in deeply until the smell started to fade. His stomach rumbled. He whined in discomfort.

He knew where her room was. She wouldn't be awake but if he could just slip in and take another...that might help quell the hunger until he could manage to fall asleep. He struggled with the thought a little longer before giving in. Edward sat up and swung his legs over the side of the bed, lingering only a few seconds longer before jumping down, his feet hitting the cold floor. He tip-toed over to his wardrobe and pulled it open, reaching inside and withdrawing a simple dressing gown. He threw it over his shoulders and pulled the belt tight, closing the wardrobe door before stepping out of his warm room and into the drafty hallway.

All of the children's bedrooms were on the same hall. Claire was still young enough to share with Emmett and Ettie. Nellie was the only one still in the nursery. Edward made his way down the long hall, his eyes slowly adjusting to the darkness. By the time he reached the nursery door he could barely make out the faint patterns of carousel horses that had long ago been painted onto the stained wood. He grasped the handle and turned it gently, opening up the door carefully so that it did not so much squeak on its hinges. As soon as he walked into the room he could hear the sound of the baby's gentle breathing, filling the otherwise stifling silence. Her bassinet was set off to the side, away from any amount of space where activity might reasonably occur. Edward felt dizzy as he took another step forward, reaching out his hand to brush his fingers over a stack of clean baby napkins. The corners of his mouth were wet. He self-consciously reached up to touch his face – was he drooling?

He shook his head, grabbing a handful of napkins and shoving them against his face, burying his nose in their depths and breathing deeply, trying to calm himself down. His stomach knotted and cramped horribly. He took another step closer to the bassinet, holding out a hand to steady himself. He grasped the satin edge, digging his fingernails into the padding. He pulled the cloth down away from his face long enough to peer down at her, and was hit full-force with that intoxicating aroma. That *something* he still couldn't place.

She was lying on her stomach, curled up underneath a baby-sized quilt. Her soft cheek rested against a tiny pillow edged with lace, her cherry red lips pursed and her breathing slow, even.

He could *hear* her heart beating. Her breathing. He placed a hand on the back of her head, touching downy dark hair. How many children died in infancy, he wondered. How many simply rolled over in the middle of the night and smothered themselves in lavender scented pillows?

She made a face and tried to roll over when she felt his hand on the back of her head. He pressed harder, holding her down so that her face was pressed between her pillow and the side of her bassinet, into a mess of blankets. She started to cry, but he did not relent. He felt himself pressing down harder, harder – just to stifle the screams.

It wasn't long before she wasn't breathing anymore.

Edward's mouth watered anew as he stroked her hair, pressing the flat of his palm to her back. He wiped his mouth with the back of his free hand and dug his fingernails into the sheer fabric of her nightdress.

He found a hole. It only took a little tug to make it bigger. His fingers hit cooling flesh, and his nails seemed to elongate on contact like a cat flexing its claws. He was less concerned about the odd occurrence and more interested in how easily they now sliced open Nellie's skin. The scent of blood hit his nose and that was it, he was in a frenzy, using both his hands to rip apart her back - chunks of tender fat at a time flying as he dug for her heart.

A pocket of muscle tore open and there they were – the rich, amber colored beads he knew existed. Edward's mouth fell open, strings of saliva dripping from his lips as he dove face-first for them, his tongue snaking out and scooping up as many as could fit at once. They were slippery and gritty and tasted better than anything. They tasted better than pastries filled with cream – better than sun-ripened berries still warm and covered in fresh sugar making them syrupy and delicious. He cried, choking on a sob with every swallow, the grim realization of his actions not enough to overcome the hunger that compelled him to keep eating – even when the entire soul was gone and there was nothing left but blood and a desecrated corpse.

Edward pulled away from the bassinet, tears still streaming down his cheeks as he licked his fingers, sucking every bit of the feast away. When he was finished he buried his face in his hands and wailed, fear and guilt wringing ragged, heartbroken sobs from his throat.

"Nellie, Nellie, Nellie..." He couldn't stop saying her name. Each time made him cry harder. He pounded his fists against the floor and screamed, unable to stop thinking about what could happen to him now. What his parents were going to say, if he would be put in jail, if he would hang...

And how wretched it was that, for the first time in months, he finally felt full.

Henry could not swallow. He could barely breathe. He stood immobile, gasping for air and fighting to get past what felt like an enormous lump in his throat. His gums ached. He could feel the vicious tips of his metal teeth trying to come up behind his human ones; their razor edges scraping against the smooth enamel. Blood and spittle that he could not expectorate gathered in his mouth.

He was staring into a cloud of grey smoke that made his eyes sting. Hot tears welled up and spilled, running down his cheeks as the thick, lazy puffs billowed into the air one right after the other – all streaming from the same foul source.

"Jahangir," a deep, dark voice growled his name. His Biblical name... he had not heard it in ages.

"Jahangir," it said again, accompanied by another cloud of smoke. "Now is the time to fall prostrate... and beg for the mercy of Hell."

That voice...he knew that voice...

The glowing orange tip of a cigarette appeared and dense, caramel-colored fingers tapped the end. Grey ash dribbled towards the ground, landing on top of Henry's shoe. Despite the circumstance, he made a face.

"All those souls," the voice admonished him. "All those damned, filthy souls. What did you do with them? Did you eat every single one? Every pathetic, quivering little jelly-like soul?"

The metal teeth pushed up further, splitting sensitive gums. Henry winced and cried out as the hand reached for his neck, gripping it hard enough that he heard bone snap and the grisly crackle of cartilage...

Henry's eyes opened and he gasped, choking on his own wet cough. His throat convulsed as he finally managed to swallow, his nose burning and his eyes still watering. He cleared his throat and coughed again, his chest heaving as he tried to catch his breath. He glanced over at Violet to see if she had been the one to wake him. She had not. In fact, she was dozing a bit herself, one elbow propped up against the wall of the carriage as she stared out the little window through half-lidded eyes. Her other hand was still resting on top of her lap, lost in the folds of her skirt. She hadn't even noticed he stirred.

Silently grateful, he looked out his own window at the uninteresting yet copious number of trees that lined the worn dirt road. The carriage jerked and jolted every now and again as they hit dips in the path, but other than that – carriage rides were the singular most boring thing human beings had ever conjured into existence.

Thankfully, by the thinning of trees, he could tell they were close to their destination.

"My dear." He reached over, touching Violet's shoulder. He saw her long lashes rise and she looked over his way, eyes glassy and cheeks flushed.

"Hm?" she asked, leaning into him a little as she stretched.

He could not help but smile, though his jaw still ached. He ran his tongue over the back of his teeth – no metal. Thankfully.

"We are nearly there." He reached up to stroke her warm cheek. She smiled at him, barely, and then straightened back up, smoothing out her skirts.

"I expect you to behave," she said, fully awake now. The atmosphere was slowly simmering back down to normal.

"I always behave!" He put a hand to his chest, insulted. He glanced out the window again, happy to see the tall, ostentatious gas lamps that marked the edge of Elliot's property.

"I mean it," she said. "Elliot wants to make a good impression on this woman."

"Then why did he invite me?"

"My guess is so that James can have someone to play with." She pulled out her drawstring purse, opening it up and pulling out a little hand mirror, lifting it high so that she could get a proper look at herself. A few strands of hair had come free from their pins and decided to slide down over her face, curling attractively around the ridges of her cheekbones. She pursed her lips in disapproval and moved them back up, securing them once more with pins in the shape of pastel-colored flowers.

The carriage hit gravel, and the large circular entryway gave them a full view of the manor. Henry sighed in relief, having regained the full of his composure and ready to forget himself in a night of drinking and eating other people's food.

The carriage came to a complete stop. Violet waited for the footman to open up the door before she stepped out. Henry followed her, straightening his cravat as he did so, nodding to the servant as they began their ascent up the front steps.

"I can make a good impression," Henry said belatedly, lifting his cane to rap the bronze head against the double doors. Violet opened her mouth to reply, but before she could the doors parted and Elliot's tall, severe butler appeared – regarding them down his nose before bowing curtly at the waist.

"Lord and Lady Clifton. Welcome," the man said. "Allow me to take your coats."

"Thank you, and well-met," Henry said, somewhat sarcastically as he slipped off his pinstriped navy coat and draped it over the man's arm.

"Lord Dosett awaits you in the billiard room," the butler said, helping Violet with her own plum-colored garment.

"With drinks, I hope," Henry said, turning to Violet and offering his hand. She accepted it, sliding her fingers over his as they started down the short hallway.

The doors to the billiard room were already open, inviting them inside with the warm glow of a blazing fireplace. James was bent over the game table, a cue sliding back and forth between his fingers, aimed at a smooth white ball.

"Good evening," James said, the cue shooting forward between his fingertips. Its blunt end popped as it hit the ball, an action which sent it spinning across the table and smashing into two more. Only then did he look up to acknowledge them, flashing a white smile.

"Good evening," Henry returned. "There had better be a cue for me on that rack."

"Help yourself," James said. "I'll start a new game."

"Where is Elliot?" Violet asked, shooting a glare of disapproval in Henry's direction.

"I'm attempting to get drunk before dinner begins," Elliot spoke up from his place near the fire, obscured almost completely by darkness so it was no wonder he had gone unseen. "It is not working."

"Might I join you?" Violet felt she would need it, if Henry intended to act like a child for the rest of the night. And he usually did.

"Help yourself." Elliot brought his wheelchair forward, closer to one of the formal chairs. Violet found the arrangement of liquors and began examining the choices.

"Where is your fiancée?" she asked conversationally, selecting a decanter of bourbon and pulling out the stopper.

"Still dressing, I assume. Possibly lingering on purpose to delay the meeting. I don't blame her." Elliot took another long drink from his glass. "I haven't told her much about either of you."

"Is she a particularly excitable girl?" Violet took her seat near Elliot, sipping from her glass.

"Excitable is not how I would frame it," James said, his ball glancing off the edge of a pocket and making him scowl. "Ever since her arrival she has become one of the most *careful* people we have ever met."

"Careful is no fun," Henry said, effortlessly sending his target ball into a pocket. "Is she afraid of stepping on Elliot's toes? So to speak."

"Maybe she just knows I don't like her," Elliot said.

"Well," Violet scoffed softly. "You've never been one to hide your feelings very well."

The room fell silent as a tread in the hallway floor creaked, signifying someone else was approaching. Everyone waited rigidly with baited breath as the newcomer appeared in the doorway, her voluptuous figure accentuated rather than hidden by the fullness of her hunter green gown.

Drucilla looked at each of them in turn, but it was Henry who arrested her gaze. He studied her eyes, noting their deep maroon color. Far more unusual than their color, however, was the lack of a ring around the iris. No thin band to clue him in as to what sort of soul she might have... which was nearly impossible for a mortal to lack. Why had James selected this woman for Elliot, if he could not see the color of her soul?

He held her gaze for too long. She was starting to blush.

He smiled at her, baring pointed canines. "Good evening, my lady," he said, straightening up and bowing. "I am William Clifton. A pleasure to meet you."

She returned his smile, an entirely insincere expression. "Lord Clifton." She curtsied. "A pleasure."

"Allow me to also introduce my wife, Lady Violet Clifton." Henry gestured in Violet's direction. She nodded a greeting, and Drucilla curtsied to her as well.

"I admit I did not know what to expect," Drucilla said, stepping further into the room and hesitantly taking a seat. "Elliot has not told me much about either of you."

"Elliot does not do very much talking," Henry said. "We actively discourage it." He looked over at James. "Your turn."

"I know," James said. "I'm thinking."

"Stalling, you mean."

"Shush!" The younger demon narrowed his eyes.

"Have you set a date for the wedding?" Violet desperately tried to steer the conversation into a more civil direction.

"As soon as possible," Elliot said. "Neither of us have much by way of family to fuss over, so it will be a modest affair."

"Every young girl's dream," Violet said, sipping her bourbon again. "Don't let Elliot coerce you into having children, whatever you do. They are most emphatically not worth it."

"Have you told Lady yet?" Henry asked James under his breath.

James shook his head, leaning over the table and muttering also to lessen his chances of being heard.

"No," he said. "I figured I would sort of … mention it when he comes by to do the monthly accounts next week."

"Another person complicates things," Henry pointed out.

"I know that!" James hissed through his teeth.

"That's not something you just drop at a monthly meeting. And a wedding? How are you going to get away with that one?"

"Are you kidding me?" James sneered. "A wedding will be the most normal thing that Elliot has done."

"Mhm." Henry watched as James went for his next shot...and missed. "I can't see the color of her soul."

"Neither can I." James straightened, looking at Henry expectantly for the demon to take his turn.

Henry stepped closer to James, his hand brushing over the back of the younger demon's hand. "She does have one, doesn't he?" he sounded concerned.

James pulled his hand back quickly as if he had been bitten. "Of course she does," he snipped. "Why wouldn't she? She is mortal, after all."

"Is she?" Henry tapped his cue against James' cheek. "Or is this entire thing an elaborate ruse to distract him from you...?"

The butler cleared his throat again. Henry and James both turned to face the door, seeing that Violet and Drucilla were starting to stand.

"Dinner is ready, my lord," the butler said, speaking directly to Elliot.

"Thank you," Elliot said, tossing a very expectant look at James.

James set his cue down on the table, turning to Henry and glowering, hissing under his breath, "There is *nothing* to distract him from!"

Henry didn't say anything, he just yipped – mimicking a lapdog as James grasped the handles of his lord's chair.

CHAPTER 13

The door to the nursery opened. Edward lifted his head, his heart slamming into his ribcage at the same time. He didn't know how much time had passed, or if his parents had already arrived home. He felt more tears begin to well up, stinging the tops of his raw cheeks.

The person who appeared in the doorway was neither his mother nor his father – not even the nursemaid. In fact, he did not recognize them as Claire until she was standing only a foot away from him in her nightshirt, her small hand bunching up her skirt in graceful fingers.

"Edward?" she asked quietly. "What's wrong?"

"Nothing," he said, ducking his head quickly.

"Bull. I can hear you crying all the way down the hall..." She knelt down beside him and took hold of his wrists, attempting to pry his sticky hands away from his face. "What happened to you?"

He looked up at her. She could just make out the dark splotches of blood on his face.

"I killed her," he whispered, his voice hoarse. "I killed her and I ate her soul." He knew that was what he had done. It sounded strange to say it, and Claire was looking at him as if he had gone mad. Nevertheless she stood, going over to the bassinet and peering over the edge at the carnage.

"Edward..." she said, her throat tight at the sight of their youngest sister, cracked open like a shellfish with the cavity behind her heart gaping empty. "What have you done?"

Edward broke down into a fresh bout of tears.

"They're going to know," he babbled, wrapping his arms around his knees. "They're going to know. Mother and Father, they... they..." He clenched his fists, his knuckles turning white. "They will take me to the police and I'll go to jail. I'll hang, Claire - they're going to kill me because I'm a murderer...!" His words trailed off into an incoherent slur as he could not contain his own gushing tears. Claire stiffened, grabbing him by the shoulder and bringing her open palm down across his face. Edward's sobs halted immediately and he choked, looking up at her stunned by the warm red mark on his cheek.

"Stay here," she said, as if he would go anywhere else. "Go through her clothes. Find something new for her to wear – whatever looks closest to that. And be quick." She left the room, and he scrambled to his feet. His knees were shaking – he had spent so long on the floor that for a moment he doubted his ability to walk. He managed to keep himself steady as he crossed the room, going to the dresser where all the baby clothes were kept and pulling open the top drawer – rifling through with bloodstained hands.

Claire reappeared not long after, carrying with her a brightly burning lamp and a little basket of sewing supplies. She went over to the bassinet immediately and lifted the corpse out of it, careful not to tip anything in the wrong direction lest blood and innards pour out onto the floor. She crinkled her nose at the smell of bile and exposed organs. Claire sat down on the floor, keeping the lamp as close as possible. She put the corpse across her lap and started going through her sewing kit, pulling out a sharp needle and very light, crème-colored thread.

"Take out all of those blankets," Claire instructed him as she threaded her needle. "Anything stained with blood. Put fresh ones in and turn the mattress over. Then go wash your hands." She placed the needle between her lips and stripped the baby down, tossing the bloody clothes to the side – the beginnings of a gory pile. Frail bones crunched as she pressed the sides of the baby's ribcage, pushing everything back into its place so she could pinch the loose skin together like a seam. She whipped her needle out from between her lips and set to work. It gleamed in the candlelight, flashing back and forth as she did her best to make the tiniest, most invisible stitches possible. Edward did as he was told and watched her work, intrigued, ending his task by going down the hall to scrub the blood from his hands, arms, and face.

He eventually returned to her, throwing his dressing gown into the bloody pile – reduced to just his nightshirt. He shivered a little as he knelt down beside her. She had tied off the stitches and was scrubbing blood away from the small corpse's pale skin with the clean edge of a stained blanket.

"Give me that dress." She nodded to the one he had picked out. He handed it to her and she sat the baby up in her lap, pulling down the dress over its lolling head. It was a surreal moment, as for a few seconds, he forgot Nellie was dead.

"Someone is going to see the seam," he said weakly, knowing he had absolutely no room to protest.

"No one is going to see it," she said. She stood up, lifting the baby with her as she did so, and set the corpse down into the cradle, covering it up with blankets and turning it back over onto its stomach so that its face was wedged between the pillow and the wall of the bassinet. "There," Claire said, breathing a sigh as she pushed her hair away from her face. "She died in her sleep."

Edward swallowed, not sure he fully comprehended what had just happened – or that he might leave this situation alive. "What do we do with all this?" He gestured to the pile.

She gave it a long look, as if she hadn't thought quite that far. "Throw it in the laundry, I guess."

"Won't that be suspicious?" Edward worried his lip. "Someone is going to notice."

"Shh," Claire dismissed, waving her hand. "I'm thinking..." She looked around, as if inspiration would spring out from a dim corner. "We will burn them."

"Burn...?"

"In the fireplace." Claire walked over to the hearth, picking up a large iron poker and prodding at the embers. A few red sparks swirled up the chimney as soon as she disturbed them, coaxing the flames back to life. "Bring them over here. Hurry."

Edward gathered the cloth up in his arms and walked over to where she was. She grabbed the bloodstained baby dress from the top of the pile and threw it in, pressing it down into the log with the poker. The smoke was already starting to increase, stinging their eyes and throats. Claire coughed and grabbed another handful of baby blankets, tossing them into the fireplace, again pressing them down and waiting for them to start burning before gesturing to Edward that he could do the same.

The smoke was unbearably thick now, and the smell particularly oppressive. Claire hacked another cough and waved her hand in front of her face, stepping back from the fireplace and letting the poker drop to the ground as she wiped her hands on her nightshirt, desperate to relieve them of smudges so she could rub at her eyes.

The flames were burning high and hot now, voraciously consuming what they had been given. Edward did not back away, though his vision was blurred by tears and his lungs felt like they were filled with smoke. He stared into the fire, his fingers twitching, his gums aching.

"We should get someone," Claire said. "It's getting bad, it could spread..." She glanced at her brother, still entranced. "Edward! Can you hear me...?" She reached out and grabbed his wrist.

She saw burning orange eyes, and pupils narrowed to cat-like slits. He hissed and his gums bled, sharp metal tips poking out from underneath his teeth. He lifted his hand and raked short claws across her cheek – leaving four ragged lacerations.

Claire's hand fell away and she clutched her cheek, her eyes wide as she turned away from him, running as fast as she could, her throat closed to a scream. She flew down the hall as if he might pursue her, but he could only stare after her, blinking slowly, wondering what he did.

His nail beds were sore and his gums felt like someone had extracted his teeth with a penknife, but he had no idea why he had screamed.

There was fresh blood on his fingertips... he remembered lifting his hand against her. Had he hurt her in some way?

The fire spat a tongue of flame up the chimney, growling and threatening to expand. He gave it a withering look and the flames simmered down, popping discontentedly but quietly – like a scolded child.

He coughed again on the smoke, rubbing his eyes with the back of his hand and blinking a few times to clear away the fuzziness that was coating his vision.

Nothing helped. He swayed on his feet. Edward attempted to take another deep breath, but only managed a series of short, rapid attempts before his eyes rolled up and he crumpled to the ground.

"Married life seems to be treating you well," James said while Henry picked at his food.

The elder demon smiled, not looking up from the neat pile of glazed salmon he had managed to shred with his fork.

"I was going to say the same for you," Henry replied cheerily.

James bared his teeth. "We do *not* act like a couple..!"

"The hell you don't."

"I do not understand your obsession with the idea."

"And I don't understand his obsession with your cock. Yet the way he looks at you one would think the Ark of the Covenant found its resting place on your ass." Henry went back to jabbing at his food, attacking the roasted vegetables next. James rolled his eyes expressively and took a long drink of wine.

"Do you think she's beautiful?" James tried desperately to switch the direction of the conversation, nodding to indicate Drucilla at the opposite end of the table.

"I wouldn't go that far," Henry said, leaning back in his seat. "She is certainly *interesting*. And interesting can trump beautiful any day if it's done well. I want to see her soul. Do you think there is such a thing as a soul without color?"

"I wonder what it would taste like," James said, staring intently at the young woman.

"Like vodka, probably," Henry responded, teasing his bottom lip with the prongs of his fork. "Wouldn't *that* be something?"

"I wonder if it would be even harsher than one as black as Elliot's," James speculated aloud.

Henry laughed under his breath. "A soul so bitter it expels all color? One could get addicted to that. Very easily."

"Well." James had to look away before he caught himself salivating at the idea. "I did not choose her for her soul."

"Why *did* you choose her?" Henry smirked. "Her beauty?"

"She was easily acquired," James muttered, refiling his wine glass. "And you know, Elliot has been getting a little bit...soft."

"I beg your pardon?"

"He's losing his edge," James said. "To put it plainly."

"Ah, I see." Henry set his fork down on his plate. "So your idea is to get him to marry and rekindle his hatred for humanity. That way he can cultivate a nice bitterness for you right before you eat his soul."

"Essentially." James drained another glass.

"I wish I could use that reasoning with Violet. 'Come on, love, let's have another child. It will make you into a better meal'."

"What do you think they're going on about?" Violet asked, leaning forward with her fingers interlaced and her chin resting on top of them.

"I'm afraid to ask," Elliot admitted.

"Do they do this often?" Drucilla asked quietly with a curious tilt of her head.

"Sometimes," Violet said, pulling her fingers apart and straightening up in her chair. "It is usually better than if they try to annoy us in closer proximity." She regarded Drucilla from behind long, dark lashes. "You were just telling us about your father."

"Ah yes...I don't think he will make it to the wedding."

"Such a shame," Violet replied. "Then again, my father did not attend my wedding either. Something about a cold."

"Oh?"

"Mm, yes. But it killed him, so I suspect it was slightly more than that. Regardless." Violet lifted her wine glass, sipping from the frail rim. "Henry and I may very well not make it, either. We have a guest that week, and there are end of the month accounts to go over."

"It will be modest," Elliot said, echoing his words from their earlier conversation. "There will be no need for a lot of fuss if you can't make it."

"Oh," Violet smiled. "I'm sure Henry will not want to miss it."

It was late when they arrived home. The gas street lamps cast yellow light and long, ominous shadows that crept up the stoop and slithered up the sides of the tall, narrow buildings. Henry stepped out of the carriage, his mind elsewhere as Violet followed his lead, her feet coming to rest on the cobblestones beside him.

"Is something the matter?" she asked him.

He didn't know. He could smell it in the air, smoke and burning cloth and blood. But the house was intact. Nothing was disturbed.

He smiled at her. "I doubt it," he said. "I'm only tired." He walked up the steps leading to their door, barely touching the doorknob as it flew back, and the nurse was standing in the entrance, her face streaked with wide, red paths of tears and her trembling bottom lip split and bleeding from having been bitten so hard.

She took her bottom lip back into her mouth to stifle the sobs that rose anew when she saw her lord. She covered her face and sank to her knees, her shoulders shaking.

"What is wrong?" Violet demanded. She stepped past Henry, bending to grab the nurse by the shoulders and shake her. "What happened? *What is wrong?*"

"The baby!" The nurse gasped out her cries, every sound coming out strangled. "The baby... Nellie... she's... she's dead!"

"Oh for the love of Christ!" Violet hissed, shoving the nurse aside to step past her.

Henry blinked. "Darling..."

"We have lost one baby before, Henry!" Violet shouted, not halting in her strides as she started up the staircase, picking up her skirts. "I don't need this girl acting like a blubbering fool...!" She was cut off as she disappeared around a corner. Henry shook himself out of his trance, following her up, taking the steps two at a time.

He caught up with her in the doorway of the nursery. When he reached her she was standing there, rigid as if she had been cut from stone. He followed her line of vision, and the bassinet was not her focus.

She dug her nails into the wooden frame so viciously he feared they might split. He took her wrist and pulled her hand away. She only jerked away from him and tossed him a dark look, as if he had broken some sort of spell by moving her, and she dashed into the room, her skirts billowing as she settled near the fireplace and took their son, Edward, into her arms.

"Water," she said, so quietly he barely heard her. Henry vanished, grabbing a startled maid and sending them for a pitcher of water. He paced in the hallway, waiting for their return, his anxiety increasing by the second. He waited long enough to see them coming up the stairs before turning back into the room and going up to the bassinet, grasping the edge, his other hand pulling back the covers.

He had seen so many dead bodies, but those of babies were something else altogether. It was entirely alien and horrible. She looked like a wax figure, all of the color drained from her cheeks and her still forming, puckering mouth as purple as a blackberry.

He took her in his arms and felt her weight. This wasn't like the first time, when the baby had died in its crib barely a few weeks after birth. That time, it hadn't felt real, weighing no more than a doll. This time, it felt like she was about to stretch out her arms and sleepily wrap them around his neck.

As a demon, he did not know how to process what he was feeling, or even register whether he was feeling at all. Was he angry? Perhaps.

Behind him, Edward coughed in his mother's arms. So only one child was dead.

Henry set the baby back down against the blankets, lifting up one of her thin eyelids just to see if the colors of her soul were bleeding in the final moment. Maybe he could taste it, if enough of it had formed. Wait until Violet went to bed, and make a long opening down the front of her chest like a seam.

Empty. The faint rings around her irises, which only days ago had not *quite* been strong enough for him to peg a color, had vanished completely.

Henry growled.

He turned away from the bassinet, nearly tripping over his wife and son, who was starting to pull himself back up to a sitting position. Edward looked over his shoulder and in that moment, he and his father locked gazes.

And just like that Henry knew. He *knew*. And he was pissed.

Edward had eaten Nellie's soul. That little shit.

Henry turned back to the baby, wondering how. He flipped her over and dragged down the collar of her dress, enough to see a few stray threads sticking up from a fleshy closure – work too clean to be Edward's. So another one of his children was involved.

Henry wasn't sure whether he should be impressed. He settled on letting that idea irritate him further.

"She smothered," Henry said, looking over at Violet, trying to soften his voice as if he cared to comfort her. "They really should post some safety regulations for such things."

"I'm sorry, father," Edward said, swallowing hard. "I was in here, but I didn't hear her...she didn't cry or anything."

"I'm sure she didn't," Henry said, approaching his son and setting a hand on the top of his head, fondling the edges of his budding horns. "They're going to fall off soon. But don't worry. They'll grow back." He knotted his fingers in Edward's brown hair. The child squeaked in pain.

Henry's blue irises were splitting apart, beams of blazing orange were filling up the empty space. Violet took notice, her breath hitching as she rose, taking hold of Henry's wrist firmly.

"Let him go," she said, her voice hard. He looked at her, but otherwise did not respond.

Blood was starting to drip from the corners of his mouth. His teeth were coming up.

"Let him *go!*" She tugged on his wrist, and he released his hold on Edward's hair only to bring her arm up and use the momentum to grab her by the throat. She sucked in a ragged gasp, freezing in place, her mouth partially opened, jugular pounding.

Every bit of her was screaming for him to rip her open, to scrape out her bitter soul and gorge himself on its divine color.

But it wasn't the time. She was not ripe for him yet.

His gums were not hurting anymore. His teeth had retracted. Each breath felt hard-won as he looked down at his son who was staring up at him, wide-eyed yet morbidly fascinated. The corners of Edward's mouth were wet...his son was salivating, sensing Henry's hunger, knowing what could happen – what *almost* happened.

Violet's child would have willingly watched a demon devour her soul...and begged for the scraps in the end.

Henry wanted to laugh. He released his hold on Violet's throat, taking her in his arms and brushing his lips over hers in a gentle kiss.

"I'm sorry, my dear," he whispered. The fear wasn't in her eyes, but it rose like steam from her skin. His nostrils flared as he inhaled the spicy bouquet of her horror, her apprehension...her aphrodisia, and her own snarling appetite whetted by the ferocity of his.

"You are not sorry," she said breathlessly in return.

"No." He placed a finger to her lips and kissed her again – as chastely as he could, given the presence of young eyes. "I'm not."

CHAPTER 14

"Women of your pallor should not wear white."

From the corner of her eye, Drucilla caught sight of James' reflection in her vanity mirror. He stood by the door, watching her intently – though feigning complete boredom as he slouched against the frame. Drucilla tried for a deep breath, but it was hindered by her tormentingly tight corset. She had only looked away a moment ago, and he had not been there then.

"What would be more suitable?" she asked tartly, lifting a strand of her thick white hair for the hairdresser to pull back and pin.

"Burgundy, I think. Or perhaps navy." James shrugged. "Most anything dark would do. White, ivory, or anything pastel will only serve to make you look ill."

Drucilla scoffed under her breath. "Thank you for your input."

"I would not go so far as to say anything would really *suit*." He spoke as if she hadn't. "But some sights are less offensive than others."

She clutched her comb, the teeth digging into her soft fingertips.

"Is there something you need?" she asked through her teeth. "As you can see, I'm quite busy."

"Elliot sent me to see if you were ready," he replied.

"Well, I am not." She held the comb up before she punctured something. She could only think that she would get great satisfaction out of driving it into the back of his skull.

The hairdresser lifted the comb from her fingers. "We only have the hair fillers left," the woman said, looking over her shoulder at James and smiling. "It will just be a few more minutes."

James nodded, watching curiously as she blended the synthetic pieces in with Drucilla's real hair through an intricate process that involved wrapping, tucking, and pinning. Drucilla endured this patiently, though she was less tolerable of James' presence. He could see her animosity building along with the tension in her shoulders as he continued to do absolutely nothing. It amused him.

"Are you prepared for tonight?" he asked innocently. By the time he spoke, Drucilla looked like she was about to explode.

Her mouth fell open and she quickly clamped it back shut, flustered by his question. He watched her fingers curl and grip the expensive fabric of her skirt, looking like she could very well rip it apart.

"That is a very insolent question," she said sharply.

"My curiosity is academic." He smiled, and held up his hands defensively. "I wonder if you have an idea of what it will be like. I myself have never *engaged*."

She flushed, clearing her throat and swatting at a stray strand of hair that the hairdresser quickly swept up.

"Well, clearly, neither have I," the young woman said. "I've...read about it, however. In novels."

A momentary rush of delight hit him as he sensed as flash of a kindred spirit. "I have never picked up a manual on the subject," he said, a little too excitedly. "There do not seem to be any proper ones."

"A manual?" She was taken off-guard by his enthusiasm, and her smile was bemused and uneasy. "Is that all you read?"

"It is the best way to obtain information," he countered.

"Haven't you ever read any fiction?" she queried. "Do you not enjoy it?"

"I prefer for my information to be as accurate as possible," he admitted. "And fiction...confuses me."

It finally caught up to her that he had more or less admitted to being a virgin. She found that surprising. From the way Elliot looked at him, she had assumed they had engaged more than once in every style of irredeemable fornication.

Perhaps James only meant he had never had sex with *women*.

"I do not think you will find what you are looking for in a manual," she responded belatedly to his remark. "Or you might, but it will all be in medical terms. And that takes the romance out of it."

James frowned. "What does romance have to do with any of it?"

Drucilla turned in her chair, the hairdresser stepping away to clean up the vanity. "What do you mean? Romance is the *point.*"

"*Children* are the point," James corrected her. "Why else would you bother?"

"Because it-!" Drucilla could not believe she was having this conversation. Her voice dropped down to a whisper. "Because it feels *wonderful.* It is pleasurable."

"How would you know?" he challenged. "You've never experienced it."

"But I have read about it!" she huffed.

"In *fiction.* Who knows what kind of details they've puffed up."

Drucilla stood, shaking out her skirts and reaching up to touch her hair carefully, as if to make sure everything was solidly in place. "Every author cannot fabricate the same details."

"Certainly they can." James was relentless. "It is called a cliché."

Drucilla let out a long, exasperated breath. "I'm ready," she said, clearly finished with the argument. "We can go down now before Elliot has a hernia."

"That would be among the last things he needs." James extended his hand. Drucilla looked at it for a moment before touching it carefully. His fingers clasped hers tightly and she startled, looking up at him quickly enough to catch little pinpricks of orange that appeared in the blue of his eyes. She found herself stepping closer, trying to bring them into focus to be sure of what she was seeing. But she blinked and they were gone, nothing but bright, endless cerulean protected by round glass lenses.

"Are you all right?" he asked, his tongue flickering in the corner of his mouth.

She nodded. "Yes..." She finally tore her own gaze away, trying her best to focus on what was ahead and ignore the burning in her cheeks.

Father Finchett had never seen such an oddly paired couple, and he had attended the royal wedding.

He could not remember the last time someone had asked him to perform a ceremony in their parlor – on a weekday – without it being some sort of elopement. Usually lords of Elliot Dosett's societal standing wanted their weddings to be grand affairs, but this was as far from 'grand' as it could possibly stretch. The parlor was scantly decorated with white and red flowers. The fireplace was cold, the ashes swept out and new logs placed on their rack – but no fire blazed. The room was lit by red and white candles arranged in polished silver candelabra; which made it very difficult to see. Father Finchett internally debated whether or not he should inform Lord Dosett of the century – in case it had slipped his lordship's mind. Even the church used lamps.

Drucilla Kerslake wore white, a poor choice. It made her skin look grey, and her hair resembled a swathe of cobwebs pulled up into a somewhat redeemable hairstyle. She brought to the priest's mind old wives' tales of banshees or of vampires risen from the grave. Her eyes were maroon, a sure sign of the Devil on top of everything else. Deceptively set in the midst of an innocent, child-like face, they bore into him with implacable umbrage.

And then there was Elliot, who was known for being irremediably odd. He wore charcoal grey for the occasion, trimmed with navy. The expression on his face was very much that of a young boy whose father was making him sit through church. At the side of his bride, she towered over his wheelchair.

Drucilla reached out to set a hand on his shoulder, but he flinched away from the contact. Her breasts rose with a short sigh and she looked at Father Finchett, expecting him to move them forward.

The only people in attendance were Lord Elliot's doctor and a young woman who was presumably a hairdresser – judging by the various combs and pins sticking out of her apron pocket. It was his understanding that more guests were to arrive later for the wedding breakfast but, as they were in mourning, had the good taste to keep themselves away for the ceremony.

Father Finchett cleared his throat, his trembling hands opening up his personal copy of the church's Book of Common Prayer. Knobby fingers turned delicate pages until he found the bookmarked passage he was searching for. He cleared his throat again and looked up, the candles creating a hazy aura around the couple. His eyes were already beginning to water with strain.

"O God of Abraham, God of Isaac, God of Jacob, bless these thy servants..."

The doctor sighed.

Father Finchett stiffened, clutching the prayer book tighter though his hands still trembled. "...and sow the seed of eternal life in their hearts; that whatsoever in thy holy Word they shall profitably learn..."

He was beginning to regret having the words memorized, as it allowed him to recite them automatically and gave his mind leave to wander, bringing to his attention all of the strange little interactions that would have gone unnoticed in a church ceremony.

He noticed how Elliot dug his fingernails into the arms of his wheelchair, shoulders tensed and posture erect. Drucilla was no better. Blood dripped down her fingers with how tightly she was gripping her bouquet. Whoever had arranged the roses had not been thorough enough to clip every thorn. A few droplets spattered on her skirt, a morbid compliment to the décor.

"...may abide in thy love until their lives' end; through Jesus Christ our Lord. Amen."

The doctor stifled a yawn, slipping his glasses off his nose to run a cloth over the lenses. The priest grew annoyed with the distraction in his peripherals and closed his eyes, leading into a prayer. When he opened them again, his eyes blurred with water – and he had to wipe them dry before turning to the next page in his book.

"Have you the ring?" he asked, sniffling and rubbing the back of his sleeve across his itching nose.

The doctor stepped forward, as did the hairdresser. The hairdresser reached out and took Drucilla's hand gently, slipping off the plain gold band from her left hand. The woman paused briefly when she noticed the blood but did not let it disrupt the ceremony, instead handing the ring to Elliot, who – under the priest's direction – slid it onto Drucilla's right hand.

A few more words were said and the ceremony was drawn to a quick conclusion. An awkward silence followed the priest's closing prayer, as if no one was quite sure how to proceed.

James broke the silence, clasping his hands together.

"I believe there is breakfast to be had," he said. "And guests soon to be arrive." He looked at father Finchett and granted him his toothiest smile. "With your permission."

Father Finchett nodded, clutching his book to his chest.

He did not like that man at all.

"I am sorry for your loss," Drucilla said, piercing the soft white slice of her bridal cake with her fork.

"It was no devastating loss," Violet said a bit coldly, stirring sugar into her tea. "Children die all the time. The Lord takes them before they get old enough for us to know them, in his infinite mercy."

Her words rang hollow, but Drucilla decided not to press.

"Are they your children?" she nodded to the small table set aside, where a boy and a girl sat quietly.

Violet nodded. "My son, Edward. My daughter, Claire. We have more at home. They were the only ones old enough to come."

"I see." Drucilla took another bite of her cake, not sure how to continue the conversation. There was a flash of silver, and from the corner of her eye she saw Violet setting something down on the table.

"A gift for you," Violet said, without looking at her.

"Thank you..." Drucilla responded quietly, touching the box before pulling it closer to her.

"Don't let James see it," Violet said, and her voice had an unusual edge. She turned her head to Drucilla, giving her a long – meaningful look.

Drucilla's light eyebrows went up. She nodded, and put the box in her lap. Hidden by the ridge of the table, she opened it to see a medical syringe and a dark glass bottle resting on a bed of green velvet.

The label on the bottle read 'Feminine Hygiene Disinfectant".

"I don't understand," she said quietly.

Violet reached over, touching the top of the lid and closing it for her. "After Elliot goes to sleep, fill up the syringe and use it to wash yourself out. I warn you though, it will burn." She sipped her tea.

"What is it for?" Drucilla asked, wincing at her own naïve words.

Violet tapped the side of her teacup with one pointed fingernail. "It is helpful to avoid conceiving. At the very least, it will stop you from having one every year. God knows."

"Thank you," Drucilla said, all of the sudden feeling her stomach turn sour. She wished her corset wasn't so tight – she was finding it very difficult in that moment to breathe. "Have you used it before?"

"Yes. And not often enough."

"Oh?" Drucilla's voice climbed higher the more nervous she became. "Did you not want children?"

"William wanted them." Violet sounded bitter. "Don't let Elliot talk you into it before you are ready. You are young, and childbirth is hell."

Drucilla nodded again, unsure of what to say.

"It might hurt a little," Violet said, beginning to sound like a mother lecturing her child. "When you are with Elliot, I mean. And you may bleed a bit too. That is to be expected. If you are in crippling amounts of pain, however, and you are bleeding profusely, insist on being taken to a doctor. A *real* doctor. Don't let James stuff a rag between your legs and tell you to sleep it off."

Drucilla was beginning to feel a little light-headed. "What kind of doctor is he?"

"The sort of doctor who learns as he goes," Violet snipped. "And who might not realize you don't have enough life for him to play around with until it's too late."

"I don't really know what the means," Drucilla responded.

"It is best you don't," Violet said. "In fact, pray you never do."

James brought the wheelchair to a stop at the side of the bed, as he did every night. He knelt before his lord, lowering the foot rests in order to take hold of Elliot's legs and slip off his shoe. Elliot endured the ritual in rigid silence, moving only to comply with James' attempts to help him from the chair and onto the bed – all the easier to assist him in undressing.

Drucilla sat on the edge of the bed, having finally abandoned her wedding dress in favor of her nightshirt. It was a relief to be able to breathe once more. She would never understand the purpose of a corset.

"There you are, my lord," James said, stepping back with Elliot's clothes thrown over his arm. "I will see you in the morning."

"I hope you do not think you are leaving," Elliot said, pulling himself further back onto the bed and resting against the headboard.

James blinked slowly. "Your pardon...?"

"You are to stay here." Elliot huffed. "What if I need you?"

James narrowed his eyes. "*Need* me?"

"You are my doctor. What if something happens to me? I could have an attack. I could *die.*"

"You are not going to die and you know it. Don't be so ridiculous."

"Is that any way to speak to your employer?" Elliot lifted his chin, glowering down at the demon from the top of his regal nose. "You will say 'yes, sir' and you will sit down and you will do your job."

James was seething. Too angry to even retort, he threw Elliot's clothes down onto the floor, spinning around and stalking over to the cushioned window seat. The demon folded his arms and glared hostilely at 'his employer'.

He was thinking very seriously of what Elliot's soul would taste like smattered on a cracker. Possibly not good enough to warrant the effort.

Possibly.

Drucilla looked at her new husband, trying to conceal her horror. "Surely, you don't mean it?" she asked.

"I do," Elliot said, unwavering.

"That is *barbaric.*" She looked at James, as if for help. He did not seem interested in alleviating her suffering when his own was so inevitable.

"I am being cautious. And I have every right to be." Elliot gave her a long look before reaching over and snuffing the candle by the side of his bed, all the better to mask his own dread.

Drucilla sighed in the dark, lingering for as long as she could. A shaft of moonlight pierced the divide of the dark velvet curtains, shooting a silver beam all the way across the room. She could just make out the outline of Elliot's body. It was at least enough so that she could approach him without fear of landing awkwardly on top.

She turned and crawled across the bed, her palms sinking into the soft feather mattress. Her nightdress dragged over the tops of his feet and brushed across his legs. She looked down at him, forcing a smile, and lowered herself to kiss him. His lips were resistant to her kiss, straight as a line.

She was resigned. If she was going to insist on any sort of passion, she was going to have to have an affair.

Drucilla kissed him again, unsure of what to do after this point. She looked down at what rested between his legs, unsure of what to make of it. Unlike what her novels had taught her to expect, his cock was thick and soft, lolling against his thigh like a roll of dough. She reached down to brush her fingers up the shaft, surprised at how supple the skin was and how easily it moved with the tips of her fingers.

Feeling brave, she wrapped her hand around it, and gave it an enthusiastic squeeze. He winced and she could hear him grate his teeth impatiently.

"Too hard," he said, his voice strained.

She flushed, loosening her grip, she began to stroke him – moving her hand up and down in slow, rhythmic motions. Gradually, he stiffened. She felt him grow in her hand and pulled away, watching the semi-erect cock flop against his stomach.

She took a deep breath and sat up straight, straddling his hips. She lifted up her skirt so that her warm, bare thighs were touching his and then she lowered herself down, reaching to take hold of his cock and pull it upright. He watched her descend, and grew harder by the minute. She brushed his head over her entrance and saw him wince again. She wasn't wet, and his dry flesh rubbing against hers could not have felt good.

Drucilla reached down with her other hand, working her fingers over her clit, sliding them between her labia and trying to work herself up. She closed her eyes and let her mind wander, eventually feeling the thick fluid gathering on her fingertips. She withdrew her hand, and then put the head of his cock to her again. This time he just closed his eyes and took a deep breath as she lowered herself down on him as far as she could go, only getting in about an inch or two. She cried out at the sensation of him being inside her, taking a moment to adjust. Motion helped. She moved up and down. He reached up and touched her thigh through her nightdress, startling her.

"Deeper," he whispered.

"I can't go deeper," she said.

"You can," he told her. "Force it." He rolled his hips, tightening his grip on her nightshirt he pulled her down, forcing her to spread her legs and take more of him inside. She bit her lip and gasped, her entire face red as she fought not to cry out again in pain.

A few minutes of strain, and then there was an audible pop and he slid all the way in, sudden and slick, she froze when she felt her hips collide with his and she stared at him, mouth partially open and lip bleeding.

He moved his hips again, encouragingly, and she slowly lifted herself up, using her knees for most of the leverage. She slid all the way up his shaft until she was nearly off and then slipped back down, repeating the motion a few times as she got used to it, and the pain ebbed away to a dull ache.

She glanced to the side, and of course James was watching. He watched as intently as any student seeing a dissection being performed. She had to look away as she picked up speed, self-conscious of how her breasts were bouncing with her motions, but glad to see Elliot's reaction – his forehead beaded with sweat, his fingers grasping desperately at the bedsheets.

And then she felt it. His warmth flooded her as he orgasmed, and then he started to wither between her thighs. She blinked and then slid off, a little confused, rolling over onto her back and waiting for him to speak.

Elliot didn't say anything. She listened as his breathing slowed and he drifted off to sleep.

Drucilla lifted her head. James was still sitting on the windowseat, and as far as she could tell he was still watching. She groaned and her head fell back against the pillow. She would have to wait for him to fall asleep or leave before putting Violet's present to use. Until then, she still ached... and unlike every novel she had read, she did not experience the same release that her husband did.

Maybe that, at least, she could fix. Pulling the covers up over her chest, Drucilla reached down and pulled up her skirt. Between her legs was warm and wet, her thighs slick with his semen, her lubrication – their sweat. Her fingers went past damp pubic hair and touched her clit, sensitive even from the minimal stimulation it had received. She closed her eyes, slipping wet fingertips over the tip, and tried to let her mind go somewhere better.

Briefly, she thought of Elliot, of what it might be like if he was at all enthusiastic or able. That yielded nothing. She thought of James next, with similar results. As a last-ditch effort, she thought of Henry – with his rakish smile and firm grip – and of what it would be like to be forced by him, or by him and James. She tried to think of being taken by both at once. Picturing them doing so against her will worked her up a bit, but it wasn't enough. Frustrated, she continued to stroke herself but without any real motivation. She let her mind wander again, going wherever it would. It meandered back to the wedding, and to the breakfast afterward.

She thought of Violet, and she gasped with the intensity of her own arousal – how suddenly receptive she was to her own touch, how fast her heart was beating.

Horrified, Drucilla withdrew her hand and turned around onto her stomach, shoving her face into her pillow and moaning.

No. No, no, no.

That was absolutely *not* going to do.

CHAPTER 15

"He made you *watch?*" Henry plucked a grape from the bowl closest to his hand, not sounding nearly as scandalized as he should have been.

"Human copulation is a most fascinating thing," James replied. "Although she didn't seem to enjoy it very much."

"I wouldn't enjoy sex with Elliot either." Henry sneered. "It doesn't sound like the most stimulating thing. Did she at least manage to get herself off afterward?"

"She attempted, but from what I observed she gave up."

"That saddens me," Henry said, popping the grape into his mouth. "You should have gone over there and given her a hand."

"I am hardly qualified to give lessons," James reminded him.

"That was a suggestive play on words, my good man." Henry sighed, as if his humor was a gift lost on the hopeless of the world. "Nevermind."

Lady set down his pen, lifting his hands to rub his face and cover his ears. "If you two don't mind. There is one *very asexual creature* you are horrifying."

"I don't happen to mind," Henry said cheerily.

"I don't know how you expect me to get these accounts straight with you two tossing vulgarities back and forth." The Unchaste sniffed unhappily, picking his pen back up and scratching out a new column in his ledger. "And just so you know, we are one short."

There was a pause.

James felt an old sense of dread being drudged up. "Oh?" he asked.

"Yes," Lady said, taking off his glasses to pinch the bridge of his nose. "Henry, you reported that your daughter died?"

"I did," Henry affirmed.

"Yet James did not report receiving any portion of her soul. And I never saw even one of her eyes. So what happened?"

"Sorry about the eyes," Henry murmured. "She didn't have a soul."

Lady gave him a dry look. "There is always a soul, Henry."

"She was too young."

"Bullshit." Lady returned his glasses to their place. "Just tell us the truth. Did you snarf it?"

"*No!*" Henry sighed, tilting his chair back so that he wobbled precariously on two legs. "It's more complicated than that. Just forget about it, all right? Move a few decimal points around...you're good at that type of thing."

"I'm already fudging. Which is how we have managed to avoid the frozen lake of Hell so far. I don't think it wise to push our luck." Lady regarded him pointedly over the rims of his glasses. "One scheme at a time, Henry. So what happened to it?"

Henry leaned forward, the front two legs of his chair returning solidly to the floor. "My son ate it."

James almost spat out his tea.

"Oh dear," Lady murmured, sliding his pen through a few rows of numbers, crossing them out to begin again. "That complicates thing. And here I thought one complication was enough." He tossed an accusatory look at James, who shrugged unashamedly.

"She's good for him," he said. "Well she's bad for him, and that's good for me."

"Yes, yes." Lady waved his pen in the air. "I heard it all earlier. But *you...!*" He swiveled his pen so that the fine nib was pointed directly at Henry. "*You* have some explaining to do."

"I have told you just about all I know," Henry replied, miffed. "He ate her soul. He killed her to do so. There, is that what you wanted to hear? I mean for Hell's sake, the boy is nearly thirteen. I should have seen this coming..."

"The problem is not that he devoured her soul, necessarily," Lady said, turning his palm outward for Henry's silence. "He is not a registered demon. You know the approval process for half-bloods is an arduous one, and there are only a handful of cases to look to for regulation guidelines. Most parents who are interested start when the child is first born, although starting at conception gets you places faster."

"I wasn't interested in registering him," Henry said, trying not to sound too short with the auditor. "Violet and I did not want that for any of our children."

"Oh?" Lady prodded. "Planning on devouring yourself, weren't you?"

Henry was silent.

"Funny, how such a callous notion comes from a demon using filthy little phrases such as 'Violet *and I*'." Lady began to start his column all over again. "This is why they advise you not to make friends with your food."

"Lady..."

"Except you've gone straight from feeding the cow out of your hand to buggering her in the stall."

"Oh for the love of Hell," James interjected. "I am nauseous as it is."

"You know nothing of my relationship with Violet," Henry growled. "Neither of you do, so just keep your mouths shut."

Lady's eyebrows went up and he set his pen down, shutting his ledger and leaning back in his chair. There was a half-filled glass of claret within his reach, and though his mouth felt parched, his stomach felt too sour to tolerate it.

"We don't have to fix this immediately," James said. "Just delay the reports. We know you can."

"I know I can, too," Lady said, more to himself than to the demons surrounding him. "I've just had a really strange feeling lately. It's a bad one...like when I walked out of Heaven, that hopeless sense of being swallowed up by Hell. Not knowing what awaits you...just knowing it feels bad."

"Then we know we can't afford to make any more mistakes." James looked at Henry. "We are going to have to do something about your boy."

"I can take care of my own family." Henry's lip curled disdainfully. "*You* focus on keeping that lord of yours on a leash."

"From what you have been telling me, he would like that too much," James flashed back.

Lady could not stay focused on the conversation. He could not shake the feeling that something was coming their way. Something dangerous.

He suddenly felt obligated to get out of the house as quickly as possible.

"Gentlemen," the Unchaste said, rising and draining his glass of claret in spite of his stomach. "I am returning to town so I can finish this and file it away. I will see you later."

Henry gave him an odd look. "Aren't you staying for dinner?"

"I shouldn't." Lady glanced down at his round little belly. "But if I have need of either of you, I will make contact. *Especially* with you." He wagged a finger at Henry. "I expect to receive a plan from you within the next two days. I am not descending into Hell on account of your poor decision to procreate."

Henry set his jaw, but did not respond. Lady swept up his ledger and his pen, setting them both down inside of his briefcase before closing it up. With a small nod, the auditor headed swiftly for the fireplace, ducking as his shoes touched the cold hearth.

He disappeared in a cold of black smoke. Henry and James exchanged looks.

"Odd behavior," James said, pouring himself another cup of tea.

"Mm." Henry rubbed his chin. "Since when is Lady not odd?"

James nodded his agreement, and that was the end of the discussion.

She was dressed inappropriately for the period. And that wasn't even considering the weather. Hindsight is 20/20 and hers was reflecting that a jacket might have been nice, or at least tights. As it was, she sat in the large over-stuffed chair, shiny calves slipping over the chilly worn brocade. She had already tried to shut the window and it didn't budge. It chose to remain partially raised, enough so that she could have stuck her whole arm out without trouble, and the thin white curtains did nothing to keep back the cold breeze that slipped through uninvited. At least her cigarette was warm. That was her only consolation.

She heard the sound of a key jamming into the apartment door's lock. The knob rattled and there was a series of harsh swear words, followed by a quick kick to the sill and another jerk on the knob. Finally, the door opened and a petite, effeminate man walked through. He swore again as he slammed the door shut, turning the lock viciously and glaring up at the jamb as if the entire structure had hindered him on purpose.

He did not even notice the woman sitting there, ashing her cigarette over a teacup saucer.

Greed sucked on the damp end of her cigarette. This could not possibly be the Unchaste she was looking for.

Lady wrinkled his nose, smelling the smoke. He unwrapped his grey scarf and tossed it over a comically short coat rack but still did not notice her presence. Greed was growing impatient.

"Good afternoon," she purred, taking another long drag so that white fumes poured from between her sultry plum-colored lips.

Lady turned slowly on his heel, pinching at the fingertips of his moleskin gloves. He recognized her – what soul in Hell did not? She was a lesser Sin, to be sure, but that did not make her any less of a force to be contended with.

He could not speak. Anything he might think to say stuck in the base of his throat. The presence of a Sin could have only meant one thing – that someone, somewhere in Hell had caught on to him.

He tried not to dwell on that. He tried to keep his mind as clear as possible.

"Good afternoon." he replied, fighting to keep his voice calm and professional. "Forgive me. I don't remember letting you in."

Well so much for that.

"I let myself in," she said, grinding out the butt of her cigarette onto the saucer and immediately pulling out one that was fresh. "You and I have much to discuss. Have a seat."

Being invited to sit in his own home was already rubbing him the wrong way. But that was what she was known for. Every space was hers. Once she was in your life, she consumed it for however long she remained.

He took a seat opposite her, perching atop a three-legged stool. She lit her cigarette and watched as he crossed his legs daintily and settled his hands in his laps, still fussing with his gloves.

"Hell paid me quite a lot of money to track you down," she finally spoke. He shivered and averted his gaze, adjusting his glasses as he took note of the goosebumps on her legs. At least she was as uncomfortable as he was. That granted him some small amount of vindictive delight.

"It was a depressingly simple task," she continued, obviously prodding him for a reaction. Lady smiled sweetly and looked back up.

"Was it? I strive to make myself available for inquiries. But you know how it is these days. The phone lines are always tied up and demons keep one running around until one's feet are bloody."

"I see."

"So they needn't have paid you so exorbitantly, as I have not been hiding." He was lying through his teeth. "I'm sure they will see it all again, however."

Greed had been audited countless times. He wished he had the pleasure of knowing what her records looked like, but that was unfortunately not his department. He was only certified for demons.

She ashed her cigarette again and he wished she would not abuse his teacup saucers like that.

"I know everything," she said. "And so does He."

Lady had to lace his fingers together to keep his hands from shaking. It was far more difficult to control his voice.

"About my latest audit?" he queried, trying to sound as dismissive as possible. "I should imagine so. The Lord of Hell always does an excellent job of staying on top of things. I've heard his employee satisfaction rates are very high..."

"What do they give you?" Her cigarette paused halfway to her lips. He swallowed.

"Ah, I'm sorry?"

"Please do not continue to play dumb with me." She finally took another drag. "I tire very quickly of games. Jahangir and Mojgan – or is it Henry Wilkes and James Highmore? However you know them. I want to know what they give you."

Lady swallowed hard. "...Eyes," he said weakly.

Amusement touched the corners of her lips. "Eyes?"

"You don't understand," he said defensively. "Your sense of taste is dulled else you might be more sympathetic. But..." He paused to conjure an analogy. "Think of how money smells to you – ink on paper, freshly minted coins – and that is how eyes taste to me."

Her smile broadened. Without hesitation, Greed reached up and touched the corner of her eye. Her sharp nail pierced the tear duct. Blood as dark as her lips trailed down her cheek as she dug her finger deeper behind her eye, finally popping it out and then offering it to him from her palm.

"Is that all it takes to train a lap dog these days?" she cooed. "A little treat?"

Lady put a hand over his mouth, staring at the eye as he forced himself to swallow and breathe.

"I shouldn't," he said, his free hand clutching the knee of his trousers. "But thank you."

He wanted nothing more than to snatch the eye from her hand and devour it, but that would be admitting defeat. He knew that if he ate it he would not make it out of this interview alive.

Greed shrugged, returning her eye to its socket. There was a horrible wet suctioning sound, and the only thing left as evidence of its removal was the crust of blood smeared underneath her tear duct.

"Gluttony must not be your patron sin," she concluded.

"No." He shook his head. "Sloth, I'm afraid... 'm dreadfully lazy."

"That explains more than it should." She slid stained fingertips up and down the length of her tight skirt. "Hell already knows where you are. I would say gather what you can and run, but that seems a moot point. By the time you reach the other end of the world, it will already have opened up. You will be swallowed in your entirety. Satan has no mercy for those who smear the corporate name."

Lady could feel all of the color draining from his face.

"You don't happen to have another one of those?" he gestured vaguely towards her discarded cigarette ends. She produced a fresh one, handing it over to him wordlessly. Lady nodded his thanks as the end began to glow and that first taste of smoky dark tobacco rolled over his tongue, followed by the faintest nip of peppermint.

Menthols. He hated them.

"So, that's it then?" He exhaled heavily, almost choking on the smoke. "I'm to sit here and wait to be dragged down to the floor of Hell?"

She was watching him, unblinking.

He took another drag, sucking it down into his lungs, feeling his throat burn. "What is the price of your help?"

A slow smile spread across her lips, but she did not reply immediately.

"I don't know what sort of use you have for mortal currency," he continued when she remained silent. "But that seems to be your language. And my demons are currently leashed to two *very* formidable estates."

Her lips parted with her smile, showing teeth.

"And what would I be expected to do?" she asked. "I will not go out of my way to be chained to Hell in your stead."

"No, no." He waved a gloved hand dismissively. "Just keep Hell at bay. Muddy the process, redirect whoever you must... I only need to buy some time so we can scrap this whole thing and run."

"Satan will find you. No matter where you go."

"Yes, I'm just hoping if I drag him in wide enough circles he will decide it isn't worth the effort of pursuit."

"It will be a lot easier on you," Greed added, "if you do not try to save the demons."

Lady paused, turning that thought over in his brain. What was keeping him tethered to Henry and James? Besides the eyes, of course. Beautiful, succulent eyes. When the jig was up, if a chain did not bind them together – what would?

Nothing, he realized. And yet he hesitated to throw them into the fire (as it were). What would he do with eternity on the lam, all alone?

It was a lot to chew on and he did not have much time.

"I'm going to at least warn them," he said, figuring that was decent middle ground.

She shrugged, as if it did not much matter.

"Do as you will," she said. He was already standing, extinguishing his cigarette to fuss with his briefcase.

"What do I need to sign?" he asked. "We haven't even discussed an exact amount."

She laughed, the very sound like the crackling of grease in a fire.

"No need for a signature," she responded. "I never neglect to collect a debt."

CHAPTER 16

Drucilla's garden was rife with purple foxglove and white gardenias, far too pure and soft a sight for Elliot's imperial estate. The terrace was its own little haven away from the mildewing walls bearing family portraits of stern elders and stiff-backed chairs that punished you for the very sin of taking a seat. Violet found herself surrounded by carefully arranged maidenhair ferns and potted ivy with sprigs of white tendrils. The message Drucilla was trying to convey was, at best, hamfisted.

The teacups had the translucency of bone china, the gold-edged lips peeled back ever-so-slightly and shaped like petals. Drucilla's dress was purple taffeta, a ghastly shade that made her pale skin looked mottled like an uncooked sausage. That was all Violet could compare her to. Meanwhile, the no doubt intentional coordination of her hostess' dress, the teacups, and the garden had a near-dizzying effect. Violet felt herself growing nauseous the longer she was forced to sit and endure the midday ritual.

'This is Hell,' Lady Clifton thought. 'Hell where the demons have had the good sense to flee.'

"Lady Clifton?" Drucilla's voice queried, sounding faint as if Violet were trying to wish it away and only partially succeeding.

Violet brought herself back, ripping her gaze away from the rows upon rows of austere foxglove that were turning her stomach sour.

"I apologize," Violet said, her words sounding strangely distorted in her own head. "I was reflecting on what you said. He made James stay?"

"And *watch*." Drucilla cradled her teacup in her palm. "It was the most humiliating ordeal I have ever suffered through."

"I doubt it was enjoyable for anyone involved," Violet said before she could stop herself. "Least of all James."

Drucilla scoffed. "I think he enjoyed it."

"I suppose I would not doubt it. He has always been keen on the misery of others."

"Ah, there you are, my dear." Henry's voice, like the bugle of a cavalry, sounded for her rescue. "I have recovered you at last."

"You are late, Lord Clifton." Violet masked her relief behind the garish rim of a teacup.

"Forgive me." He bent to kiss the back of her lace-covered hand. "I was detained, of all things, by a witness."

"A witness...?" Drucilla prompted him to elaborate.

"Yes, one of those..." Henry waved his hand airily as he searched for the word he was looking for. Unable to find it, he plucked a cucumber slice from its tray on the table and popped it into his mouth. He flipped his coattails back, taking his seat and reaching for another. "I'm not sure what else to call him. I don't know how he got in.

Maybe the gardener let him in or maybe he hopped the gate, I'm not sure. At any rate, he asked me if I was a Christian."

Violet snorted. "That's a ridiculous question."

"Indeed," Drucilla agreed. "What did you tell him?"

"I told him that I had conversed with the Almighty personally and did not think very highly of Him."

Violet smacked him solidly in the arm. Henry flashed a grin and began to make his tea.

"No," he laughed. "I said of course I knew God. And then we had a short discussion. He seemed disappointed that he could not convert me. I told him he should try to work on Elliot."

Drucilla had to cover her mouth with her hand to keep from laughing out loud. "Let us pray the boy doesn't actually find him."

"James will send him packing, I'm sure of it." Henry stirred milk and honey into his tea. "But then, James knows more about Heaven than I."

"I have always wondered about Heaven," Drucilla said. "Famous paintings and liturgical works do not seem to do it justice."

"And Hell, also," Violet chimed in, watching Henry take his first sip of tea. "If it is full of horrors as some claim."

"Assuming either exist," Henry replied candidly. "I am far more interested in the world between."

Violet kept her eyes on Drucilla, interested in the other woman's reaction. Henry's manner of speaking suggested that he had first-hand experience of whatever he spoke. In this case, he did, but Drucilla would not know that.

"What in-between?" Drucilla ran her spoon around the inside of her empty teacup, half-interested in what he was saying, mostly contemplating more tea.

"The Netherearth?" he laughed boyishly. "As the ungodly call it. I've read about it in old texts, you know the type – the ones the church would rather you forget."

"The ones commonly burned for heresy," she responded flatly.

"Of course," he said, "but these are kept by the church in its own library – is that not interesting? You know, of course, that when a soul dies it is sent to Heaven or Hell based on the quality of its virtues or sins. But where does a soul go, when it is devoured?"

"Devoured?" Drucilla was rapidly losing all interest in the conversation. She lifted her teapot, tipping it over her cup.

"It is banished to the in-between, the upside-down. If Heaven and Hell are cogs in a great cosmic machine then the netherworld is the oil that keeps them turning." Henry turned his eyes towards Violet, his smile lethargic and predatory. "For a soul devoured, there is no judgment, no afterlife. There is only darkness. Eternity is a long stretch of cold, isolated darkness. Agonizing loneliness spent recalling every misery – every stab of guilt, every anxious thought. Those consumed by demons become nothing more than wailing memories drifting in the Netherearth... in-between life and death, shimmering white mists that chill you to the bone; sometimes they manifest as the voice you think you hear calling your name before you realize –

it was no one after all. That is what you will be. You will be *no one.*"

Violet's throat convulsed with a hard swallow. She remained frozen in her place, her lips slightly parted as if the next portion of her thought was refusing to be summoned. After what seemed like an eternity he broke the eye contact, turning back to Drucilla who had also paused in making her tea. Except she seemed far more troubled by Violet's reaction than by his words.

"Violet?" Drucilla whispered. "Are you all right, dear?"

Violet's words were a wet choke. She lifted her teacup to her lips, draining it before attempting to reply a second time.

"I'm fine," she said, setting her teacup down. "I'm feeling a little giddy. It might be the flowers." She glanced at Henry. "If our hostess would be kind enough to excuse us, I should like to lay down."

"Of course," Drucilla said. "Would you like me to...?"

"No." Violet forced a smile. "Henry can manage."

Taking his cue, Henry stood, offering her his hand. She accepted it, and he pulled her to her feet. With a nod to their hostess, he began walking with her towards the house.

"I have upset you," he said quietly, his voice low. He did not sound particularly apologetic.

"I had been looking for an out for nearly an hour. You were taking too long to leave." She stepped into the side entrance with him, he held the door open so she could gather up her skirts. "I am not cut out for the company of other women."

"So I have come to notice," he mused, following her. "Over our many years."

"Not *so* many," she was quick to correct him.

"Longer than I ever thought I would be willing to wait," he said, reaching out to take her hand once more, "for a soul as acerbic as yours."

"Then why don't you take it?" she snapped suddenly. "Instead of salivating over it like some dog forbidden from his master's table?"

He paused, an odd look crossing his face. She felt his resistance and tugged on his hand, annoyed.

"What?" she demanded.

"Why would you say something like that?" he asked oddly.

She pressed her lips together and shrugged. "You are always griping how hungry you are – how the souls you consume do not fill the void that mine will. Well you've been hungry for thirteen years now and there are no signs of us coming to an end."

He groaned. He looked away, trying to pull his hand free of hers. She didn't let him, tightening her grip on his fingers.

"How am I supposed to know when you will see fit to rip out my soul? Will my children be grown? Will I be old, or will you choose to take me when I am still moderately youthful in my appearance? I want to know...!" She lowered her voice so as not to be overheard, but was no less avid. "What is important to you – what flavors are cultivating inside me right now, and how may I combat them so I will never be appealing *enough*, never quite ripe for your harvest?"

He sneered. "My dear, if you were any riper you would be rotten. I would consider you to be in *prime* condition for plucking." He ripped his hand away, placing his fingers to his temples to massage them deeply. "Don't do this now. Don't be tiresome. Things were going so well..."

"So well...? You are an arrogant imbecile," she spat. "And you do not care about me at all. You cannot see past the terms of your contract."

She was baiting him for something. She wanted an admission. She wasn't going to get it.

"*Yes!*" A spark of rage lit up his eyes. "That is exactly all I care about. Was anything omitted from the fine print? Was there some form of misunderstanding when you signed the goddamned thing? Honestly - thirteen years of matrimony and five children later, and I'd have thought you would be *begging* for death! Most sane women would be!"

"You cannot honestly expect," she retorted spitefully, "that you can sit there and talk of Heaven and Hell and the 'in-between', about how there is no afterlife for the devoured... and expect me not to break under that revelation. It wasn't just now, you've been wearing me down for *years*. And that display just now was ghastly enough to make question this whole ordeal."

"Well I hate to be the one to inform you that it is too late, *far* too late, for any sort of regrets." He shook his head, driving his fingers upward into his hair. "You were, you *are*, an extraordinary woman. That is part of your appeal. Your vicious nature makes my mouth water. I will always uphold you in my mind as the meal I relished most. But that is where it all ends... as sweet as it is for you to pretend to care about your children and whether or not they will have the burden of caring for you in your old age. As endearing as it is for you to feign naivety, to try and make me believe that you ever thought your soul would do anything other than dissipate into darkness. I cannot love you, I am incapable of love, I am a *demon* – accept it, and do not exasperate me in your final days by trying to milk me for a different answer."

"Are these my final days?" She stepped closer to him, her voice a dangerous growl. "Is that your official warning?"

He held her gaze, wanting nothing more in that moment than to rip out her throat – to pull her soul through the opening on a thick rope of nerves.

"My only warning," he said, "is that if you wish to experience Hell, I can accommodate you – and gladly."

Whether it was the look in his eyes or his voice, she took a step back. She dropped her gaze, and for the first time since he had known her, he saw the color fade from her cheeks – a flush of anger quickly replaced by a pallor white as wax. She looked, briefly, like she might faint.

"I need to lie down," she muttered. "You are exhausting."

His chest felt tight. Henry fought the urge to reach out to her, take her in his arms and apologize. It was a ritual he had developed over the years, the most human thing he had ever brought himself to do. He was so used to comforting her, but now he wasn't even sure if she would stand for his coddling. Was it best to let things settle on their own, wean her off his affection? Would it muddy the waters further if he just apologized and said he was wrong?

Would she believe him? No, but there was something to be said for the practice itself. The motions, even the illusion of caring, had become almost more important to her than any legitimate love.

He understood this, and accepted it. She was human. She needed things he did not.

But he needed her soul dark – and he admittedly had spent a lot of time worrying about whether or not their moderately blissful life together had softened her. This outburst of hers had driven a rare fear into his core – because she had proven him right.

He let her go, and could see the hurt feelings, the dim glow of anger, festering within her.

Good.

God had always considered aviators to be one of his better designs.

But of course, the only person in existence with an appreciation for aviators *would* be the guy who created them. Satan though they were disgusting. He would have started a war in Heaven on that opinion alone, but settled for more passive aggressive methods.

In the way a Renaissance artist may have painted the face of a problematic pope onto a dog's ass, Satan made certain that aviator sunglasses graced the noses of nearly every world dictator since it had become a reasonable trend.

Now he saw his own face being reflected by dark mirror lenses. He wanted to smash them in, and possibly also smear the smug smile underneath them all over their wearer's face.

"It isn't as if I don't know what you are thinking," God said. Satan shook his head, clearing the angry red haze from his brain.

"You haven't been able to see into my thoughts for at least two thousand years," Satan snapped, waving the file in front of the Almighty's face. "I know that pisses you off more than anything. But you know what gets *my* goat?"

God shrugged.

"Asinine corporate fuckery that wastes *my* time – and yours – and others' who are involved!"

"I'm sure I don't know what you mean," the Almighty said sardonically.

Satan gripped the sides of the file, pulling it open with such ferocity that he nearly ripped it in two. "Meriwether Hayward."

"Oh," God groaned.

"Tell me this is a misprint, or that Raziel is in on some great cosmic joke..."

"Where is Michael...?" God demanded.

"I want to hear you say it. I want to hear from your own stupid mouth why you sent that angel into Hell."

God set his impossibly even teeth.

"*Say it.*" Satan loomed over the Almighty, his sub-zero shadow raising chill bumps on usually flawless tan skin.

God growled. "Meriwether ... displaced something that was very valuable to me."

"I'm going to rip off your arms."

"He lost my golf clubs – and they were monogrammed!" God whipped off his sunglasses, his voice deepening. "Thou shalt not *try exceedingly the Lord thy God...*"

"Oh cut the shit." Satan stepped back, smashing the two sides of the folder back together and cramming it back into his jacket.

"You have a lot of gall, how many times do you have to be thrown out before you realize you are not welcome?"

"I don't come up here because I feel welcome. I come up here because your office doesn't know how to send a fax." Satan looked the Almighty up and down. "And your security sucks. But this is the last you will see of me for a while. I am going to be down on Mortal Earth, cleaning up *your* mess. As always. *Ped drod.*"

He vanished, and God – in his usual manner – sulked.

Nothing had been going his way as of late. Maybe it was time for a new epidemic.

Cholera sounded promising.

CHAPTER 17

The medicine case rattled as James set it down on top of the table. He flipped open the locks with practiced ease, muscle-memory guiding his actions as he pulled out a half-filled bottle of morphine and held it up to the light, scrutinizing its contents through thick dark glass.

"You might as well put that back." Elliot dark voice interrupted his process. Long enough, at least, to make him look over at the desk where the young lord was sitting.

"Don't be ridiculous," James said, setting the bottle down and preparing a needle. "It is your medicine."

"I am crippled, not blind. And I have decided I am not going to take it. I don't need it." Elliot slammed his ledger shut, cutting the demon a challenging look. "It isn't as though I will die without it."

An annoyed look flitted across James' aristocratic features. "Certainly not. It may not lengthen your lifespan but it does quiet you down a good deal. If I could give you better temperament instead of years every time I harvested a soul I would."

"You have some gall, speaking to me in such a manner."

James' eye ticked and he drew back the syringe, carefully measuring the dose even if his strongest desire was to pour the entire bottle down Elliot's throat.

"Do I?" James asked, trying to keep his tone under control. "I was not aware that there was any form of behavioral expectation placed on me. When did this develop?"

"It has always existed," Elliot said haughtily. "Ever since we signed the contract. You are my servant and I am your lord – or have you forgotten that?"

The medicine case snapped shut. James turned around, holding the needle aloft and pushing up on the syringe, squeezing out the last of the air bubbles until nothing but beads of liquid were spilling over the side.

"Indeed, you are wrong," James said. "I am, and always have been, your *doctor.* You are my *patient.*" He looked at Elliot and smiled callously. "And you will take your medicine as you have done, without complaint. I know what is best, after all."

"You are no doctor," Elliot said through his teeth. "An overnight briefing of medical journals does not a professional make."

"You never specified that I should be professional. You merely asked I be efficient." James stepped closer until he was behind Elliot's chair, wedging his foot behind one of the wheels so the lord could not back up while the presence of the desk prevented him from moving forward. "Arm. Or are you going to force me to manhandle you?"

Elliot said nothing. He turned his head to glance over his shoulder at James, challenging him with a look.

James' smile did not wither, but it did lose any glimmer of levity. He slammed his other foot behind the second wheel of Elliot's chair, grabbing hold of his lord by a fistful of thick black hair. He wrenched Elliot's head back and pressed his mouth the young man's ear, his voice a deep, savage growl.

"Don't. Move," the demon said. Elliot froze in place, his hands pressed against the arms of his wheelchair. He felt a pinch on his neck, and the morphine burned as it entered his bloodstream – momentary pain quickly giving way to the drug's familiar sleepy golden haze.

James withdrew the needle slowly, ruefully. He released his hold on the young lord, shoving his head forward as he stepped away from the chair and went to return the needle to its case.

Elliot reached up lethargically, rubbing the injection site. "You know, I thought you had to comply with my orders, no matter what?"

"No," James said. "Shall I pull up the contract and review the terms with you? I am under no obligation to do anything I don't care to do unless it benefits our mutual goal. And shoving you around does nothing to hinder me from taking your soul. Poor marital sex is not an excuse for this type of behavior. I like to think I deserve marginally better from you, though I don't expect it."

Elliot was already starting to feel dizzy from the morphine. He gripped his wheels, turning them while he still had the strength to do so and backing away from his desk. "I don't want to talk about it."

"You were not so shy about it last night."

"Your presence was a requirement in the event of an emergency," Elliot said, giving up on movement and letting his hands fall into his lap. "You could have done the decent thing and looked away."

"But I would have missed the expression on your face when you saw the disappointment on hers."

Elliot sneered. "It is impossible to please a woman that large."

"Somehow I don't think it was *her* size posing a problem."

Elliot started to say something else, but the medication was overtaking him quickly. His head lolled and James sighed. The demon took hold of the wheelchair handles and started pushing Elliot out the door, heading down the hall towards the lord's bedroom for an unscheduled midday rest.

"You're so cruel to me," Elliot muttered, barely able to lift his chin when the wheelchair stopped and James knelt in front of him to loosen his cravat.

"You are sensitive," James said disdainfully. "That is all."

"I try so hard." Elliot reached up and took hold of James' wrist. James looked down, considering whether or not he could easily break the contact. Elliot's grip was loose. James brushed the lord's fingers away and continued his routine. He shoved his hands underneath Elliot's arms, lifting him from the chair and aiding his journey to the bed. Elliot sat down heavily on the edge and James knelt again, pulling off the lord's shoes.

"How long will I be asleep?" Elliot asked, his words starting to slur together.

"Not long enough." James placed the shoes neatly by the bed and picked up Elliot's legs, turning him so that he could lay down on the bed with better ease.

The demon tried to pull away, but to his exasperation Elliot was still clinging, his fingers clutching the lapel of James' white doctor coat.

"Stay," Elliot said.

James blinked, not quite processing the command. "Why?"

"Stay," Elliot repeated, his fingers already falling away and his voice softening. His eyelids drooped, sleep weighing them down. "Sleep with me."

James did not know whether to laugh or recoil. He leaned over, closer to Elliot, until their foreheads were touching.

"You are supposed to be bitter," the demon said. "Not vulnerable." He pulled away, straightening his coat. "We are going to have to re-examine your medication."

Elliot didn't reply. He was too far gone in his sleep.

"Sometimes, I think you are just as bad as Henry."

James turned around at the sound of Lady's voice. The diminutive Unchaste has appeared from seemingly nowhere and was now seated on a plush ottoman, his ankles primly crossed. James reached up to adjust his glasses, but did not move beyond that. He lifted his clear second and third eyelids – they slipped out of sync with each other over his eyes as he tried to re-calibrate. Speaking with Elliot always put him in a mood, and it was far more refreshing to address another spiritual entity while peering through the monochrome lenses of his demonic sight. The colors of mortal earth were too bright and frequently gave him headaches.

"If you are conflating my behavior and his towards our contractual obligations, I will be very displeased," the demon doctor said.

"Granted, you are not married to yours," Lady allowed. "Though you might as well be."

"Does this conversation have a direction, angel, or did you just appear to goad me out of habit?"

Lady balked at being referred to as an outright 'angel'. "I came to warn you," he said after taking a moment to get his wits back together. "I received a very..." Lady paused to figure out how best to phrase it. "...Ominous visitor. Our conversation amounted to this: the jig is up. Hell knows all. Cut your losses, devour your final prey, and flee. Or the Devil will find you and throw acid in your eyes as you face the madness of eternity."

James froze. "That is an exaggeration?"

"I wish it was," Lady replied grimly. "But I have seen it happen – the Devil will rip out your eyelids, including the one that can see into eternity. With that gone, there will only be a void – and no one will ever know what you see. Because they will not be able to discern words over your screams. And if the madness does not blind you, Satan will. He will throw acid *in your eyes.*" He dragged out the last three words for emphasis. "He will seal the horrors in as the last thing you ever see. And then he will anchor you to the floor of the Ninth circle and bury you up to your neck in ice. Is that how you pictured spending the next ten thousand years?"

James shook his head. He was doing his best to remain calm, but he felt like someone had stabbed him in the chest with an icepick. It had been a while since his anxiety had hit him with such crushing force.

"I have to warn Henry," the demon said.

Lady shrugged.

"Up to you," he said. "I consider my work here done. I am going to leave town as soon as possible – I consider myself at more of a risk than either of you. In fact, I am heading to my apartment within the hour. Once Francis arrives, we're both leaving."

"Where are you going?" James asked, already shedding his doctor's coat. Suddenly, he felt very hot.

"Another time, another era. Far away from this one." Lady shrugged. "I'm not going to tell you. In the event that you are caught, I don't want them to give them the ability to siphon that information from your head."

James hesitated. "Thanks?"

"I do my part." Lady stood. "If I never see you again, I wish you luck. As far as demons go you're not the worst I have ever met."

James realized that was as close to sentimental as he was going to get. He extended his hand. "You've been top notch."

Lady considered the offered hand and then accepted it. He used his grip to pull James closer, holding onto him for an extra beat. "Ditch Henry, if you have to," Lady whispered. "Remember that you don't owe him anything."

"I'll remember your warning about the lake of ice," James promised. "That is my motivator."

"Good man." Lady released him. "Ciao." He walked away, heading for the fireplace.

James watched him go. A mounting sense of dread and urgency was settling into his stomach, making him feel nauseous. He looked over at Elliot. Even if he wanted to take the young lord's soul at that moment, he couldn't do it. He would have just thrown it up.

He absolutely had to warn Henry. That oblivious ass would never make it out on his own.

When Elliot woke up he was alone. His eyelids felt heavy, as they always did when he woke up after a dose of morphine. His head was pounding, and he was not altogether too sure of the time. The curtains were drawn and all of his candles had been reduced to dim, barely glowing flames in wax puddles.

"James?" He sat up, sliding his hand over his face and trying to rip out the last of the grogginess. There was no response from the surrounding darkness.

"...James?" Elliot's voice was more of a whisper the second time around. He shoved his hands underneath his thighs and tried to pull his legs around. It had been a long time since he had tried to move himself, and now he was finding it exceptionally difficult. Stubbornly, Elliot continued to inch his legs slowly across the bed. The covers bunched up in his path and most of them tumbled off the bed, but he finally managed to drag his legs over the side. His ankles hit the wooden frame with a dull thud. Elliot leaned over, panting with the effort of moving so much as he tried to look for his wheelchair. His chest ached like he was trying to breathe underwater. His movements were all so slow...each one at a fourth of the pace he felt they should be. He kept expecting to see James approach the bed, mumbling some excuse as to why he had been late, or sitting by the fire – watching.

Yet it was becoming very clear that James was not in the room, and had not been for hours.

He could see the outline of his wheelchair. It was close to the bed, but not close enough for him to reach out and pull it over. He was going to have to find some way to get across the floor and pull himself into the seat. Elliot grit his teeth, looking down at the floor and trying to remember how long it had been since he had done any of his leg therapy. He probably had not tried to walk since they had taken him off his air tank.

Elliot dug his palms into the bed, pushing himself even close to the edge. He was already exhausted, but he was determined to make it to his chair. Somewhere, in the fog of his brain, he was convinced that if he did not move *now* then no one would ever find him. It did not occur to him that James would ever, eventually, come *back.*

His bare feet brushed against the floor. It felt strange, like his legs had fallen asleep. He could only register the faintest of sensations. With another small push his heels were against the floor and he was standing, though still leaning heavily against the bed. Elliot stood up straight and took a deep breath, slowly pulling his hands away from the mattress edge. His legs trembled slightly, but that was about it. He lifted his head and faced his chair, a faint smile tugging at the corners of his lips. Elliot fixed his eyes on his goal and took one small yet confident step forward.

The floor rose up to greet him. Elliot tried to throw out his hands to catch himself, but he did not quite make it. He landed on his face and hot blood spurted from his nose, gushing down his mouth and chin. Elliot yelled in pain and pressed his hand to his nose, trying to stop the blood from flowing between his fingers as he attempted to push himself into an upright position. His palms were too slick with sweat and blood. They ended up slipping on the floor, and he almost hit it with his face a second time.

"James!" Elliot growled, balling his hand up into a fist and smashing it against the floor. "Where in *hell* are you?"

The door opened. Elliot looked up, straining his neck to focus on the sliver of light that had appeared. He saw the hem of a tartan skirt being kicked up by very expensive, if leaning towards practical, heeled boots.

"Elliot?" Drucilla's voice carried. She held up her lamp higher; it illuminated her pale face. Elliot considered just dying on the floor instead of announcing his presence, but that seemed a little too petty.

"Here," he croaked. Drucilla cast her light his way – immediately catching flashes of bright red blood.

"Elliot! What have you done to yourself?" She sounded like chiding mother, kneeling down by his side and pushing his wheelchair out of the way so she could tend to him.

"Never mind how," Elliot snarled. "Get James."

"I don't know where he is," she replied. "I'll fetch another doctor."

"I want *James!*" His snarl was turning into a growl. "Where is he?"

"I will fetch you a *real* doctor." She started to stand. Elliot grabbed onto her skirts and pulled her back down. He grabbed her sleeve and used it as leverage to pull himself into a sitting position, but even then he did not let go.

He had to take several deep, slow breaths – staring her down like a feral animal caught in a cage.

"I'm fine," he said after a moment, fighting to quell the tremor in his voice. "It is only a bloody nose."

"You could have broken something..." she insisted.

"I didn't fall that far. And I still would have felt it." Another deep breath – he could do this. He was getting more confident in his upright position, but he still did not release her.

"Do you know where James is?" he asked.

"No," Drucilla said. "I saw him vanish down the hallway a few hours ago. I would not be surprised if he and that rogue of Violet's disappeared together. Who knows what unspeakable things they do in private. They always struck me as odd."

Elliot felt a sharp pinch of jealousy. "Is it time for supper yet?"

"I was coming up to see if you intended to dine with us." She started untangling herself from his grip. "I guess I'm glad I did."

"Help me up," he said, even though she was already doing so. Drucilla reached out and grabbed the footrest of his wheelchair, pulling it back over and then helping him back into its seat. It took several minutes, but Elliot finally settled into his chair. Drucilla made sure he was arranged comfortably, getting down on her knees to take hold of his feet before realizing... "You're not dressed."

Elliot looked down. "Damn it," he whispered under his breath. "Get my dressing gown from the wardrobe. And a blanket."

"That is hardly proper dinner attire," she said, even as she went to do what she was told.

"It is either that or you can dress me. And I would rather not be here for another hour."

"I can send a servant after James," Drucilla said. "If you're very worried."

"No." Elliot's eyes flashed and he lied through his teeth. "I don't care."

CHAPTER 18

A ledger and a handful of teabags - that was all Lady had managed to pack so far. He stepped back from the briefcase, rubbing his chin as he looked around the bare apartment. There had to be something else he would require as far as necessities. It did not seem much like a getaway if there was nothing to dramatically haul down three flights of stairs and then abandon mid-alleyway.

"Are you ready to go, boss?"

Lady looked up towards the ceiling, closing his eyes and putting a hand on top of his chest.

"Frank. I'm saving your life."

"Yes..."

"In such a case, it is bad courtesy to take mine by giving me a heart attack." Lady cast a cogitative look at his various hat boxes. "If we are going to live together, you know, there have to be some ground rules."

"I'm sorry." Francis shuffled forward with his own bag, looking down at the briefcase resting on the rigid mattress. The bed was very firmly built for only one person. The addition of anything even as large as a cat would have been near impossible. "Is that all you are bringing?"

"I'm *thinking.*" Lady started going through his drawers. There was nothing he owned clothes-wise that could not be easily replaced. Besides, he was considering a more feminine aesthetic. "None of this is necessary. This does not feel like much of an abscondment. I am very disappointed in us."

"I'm sorry," Francis apologized again. He wasn't sure why they were bothering to linger – or how Lady could not possibly feel rushed. His boss' message down to Hell had been something along the lines of *'get your ass up here while you still have one to haul'*. Francis had unplugged the answering machine and thrown anything that could possibly be considered incriminating into a bag before rushing up to mortal earth as fast as a fireplace could send him.

He had hoped Lady would be ready. That had, of course, been a vain fantasy. Francis could have taken his sweet time leaving Hell. He could have cleaned things up, burned the documents, had a nice cup of coffee or two, and have come to mortal earth much later – probably only to find Lady in this exact same predicament. The Unchaste was now sorting through his shoes.

"Boss..." Francis glanced at his watch.

"I can't believe how many of these were pushed up into a corner," Lady said. "Poor things...!"

"Boss," Francis tapped the glass.

"Do you even know how important shoes *are,* Frank?"

"I get it," Francis said. "But we really ought to..."

"I feel like you are rushing me." Lady glanced at him accusingly. "I do not appreciate that from you."

"You told me to get out of Hell and so I flew out of there like it was on my heels. I did not know 'we are about to be butchered alive' was code for 'come early enough to help me sort through the closet'."

Lady pressed his lips together and chucked a polished white Oxford at Francis' head. "You are a terrible husband, I'm sending you back."

"Husband?" Francis blinked. "I don't...?"

"I imagine that you would be the type to bring it up, sooner or later," Lady said, disgruntled. "Unable to bear sharing the same living arrangements with a lady before begging her hand in marriage due to both propinquity and propriety. So I just beat you to the punch. I imagined that you asked, and I accepted, only because you fold my laundry passably well and I do not feel like educating another fool on how I take my coffee."

"So does this mean...?" Francis was trying desperately to keep up.

"No, you are not to touch me in any way. Ever. And no, we are not going to sleep in the same bed. If you insist on touching me, I will permit a brisk handshake after coffee is exchanged in the morning. You will keep your gestures congenial with no hints of intimacy or lecherous intent. Violate these rules, and I'm sending you back to Hell with bricks in your pockets."

Francis did not know how to respond. He was still trying to wrap his head around the address of 'husband'.

"Now." Lady looked up, clacking two different shoes together. "Sensible flats, or this slightly more elegant platform? I must admit. Flats are far more versatile, but the heel is *quite* distinguishing."

"I don't know," Francis said, giving up. "I like them both?"

Lady sighed and chucked both pairs of shoes into a suitcase. "Your lack of enthusiasm is disheartening."

"I'm sorry." Francis truly regretted his inability to process anything the Unchaste was saying.

"Have you decided where we are going?" Lady had left Francis in charge of all of the destination arrangements. Francis nodded and pulled a neatly folded square of paper from his blazer pocket.

"It is a bit of a gamble," Francis said. "But hopefully it will be the last place the Devil thinks to look."

Lady nodded his head thoughtfully, a sober silence settling between the two of them. The Unchaste finished packing and then fastened the buckles on the suitcase, standing up and brushing off the knees of his trousers.

"I don't need the rest," he said. "You will buy me new clothes when we have settled in."

Francis picked up one of the bags, amused. "I will?"

"Do not ask stupid questions, Frank." Lady straightened his tie rigidly. "It does not become you."

Francis ducked his head. He picked up the other suitcase, noting the remarkable weightiness. He kept a stiff upper lip about it and started towards the fireplace. Lady followed him, pulling on his coat.

"Will I need a scarf?" Lady asked, even as Francis stepped into the flames.

"I don't know." Francis' words were already started to be drowned out by the roar of the flames. "Probably."

"Gone..." Henry touched his chin.

"From what I understand, he left as soon as he gave me the news." James leaned forward. "We don't have long."

Henry shook his head. "What does it tell you, James, that an Unchaste flew the coop faster than a candle can flicker out?"

"It tells me that we are in some deep, deep shit." James leaned forward. "And if we don't clean up our mess, collect on our contracts, and hotfoot it out of here... we are going to have Hell demanding its due. And neither of us have a thing to give."

"All I have to give to them is *you*," Henry said, chewing on the tip of his thumbnail. "And I need you around for my own purposes."

James looked at him oddly but chose not to explore that statement.

"We need a plan," Henry said.

"We are good at those," James added dryly.

Henry waved his hand, scowling. "Do not be snippy, not at a time like this. How long do you think we have?"

"Hours. Less than."

"Then the children should go first."

James shrugged. "They do not need to be savored?"

"No," Henry said. "But they need to be taken care of. I regret that I cannot leave them alive, but..." He trailed off and sighed, raking a hand through his messy blonde hair. "This is going to be more complicated than I thought."

"Have you never gorged yourself on this scale?" James found it hard to believe of the elder demon. He stood and went to Henry's side, touching his agitated companion on the shoulder. "Stop fidgeting."

"I can't help it," Henry replied.

"It is not going to be as difficult as you think," James reassured him. "What are you afraid of?"

Henry thought about it for a moment.

"Nothing, I suppose." He glanced down at James' hand, then looked up to meet the younger demon's eyes. "Where do we re-convene?"

"We will plan to meet at your house in the city," James said. "If one of us accomplishes our work here before the other, we will go straight there."

"It sounds like a plan." Henry sighed. "I had hoped for a little more time, you know?"

"I know." James was thinking about the bitterness cultivating in Elliot's soul, about how it was nowhere near its prime. "As did I."

CHAPTER 19

The night an angel came for Lady Clifton's soul, it had not rained in several hours. She had not even noticed when the thin droplets had ceased to slide down the thick glass panes, even though their fingers tapping against the sill had been thunderous enough to drown out the crackling flames in her hearth.

She was far too consumed by her own thoughts. Her needlework rested in her lap, long abandoned. She had not worked on it for weeks. It had never appealed to her, but every now and then it kept her hands busy. The needle had made a nice, permanent hole where it had sat too long pushed through the same space of muslin. It had been threaded a while ago, and the crimson strand still fell across the blank crème-colored canvas, hopeful of one day being turned into a peony, or a young girl's slipper.

Personally, Violet thought it looked a little too much like blood. A splash of dark, hot blood pumping straight from an artery. Every time she thought about it, her hands froze and she couldn't even bring herself to touch the embroidery hoop. It took her several minutes to rip her gaze away, and then she would go back to staring in the fireplace. This had been going on for the better part of the night, ever since she started thinking about Henry.

The fire was beginning to dwindle and she hadn't even noticed. In fact, she did not hear the door to the study open – though it creaked something awful and the intruder swore as he stubbed his small toe against the jamb.

Michael's first thought was that she didn't look like a woman who was on the verge of collapse. A demon had been latched onto her for over twelve years and she had not yet been reduced to a dry husk of a person. She was a bit gaunt in the face, yes, and her flinty eyes seemed shrouded by her curved noble brow. She was as pale as winter, but not cadaverous or ashen. She was not a *wasted* woman. But she was severe. He had no way of knowing the best method of getting her attention. He considered touching her arm, but he was afraid he might lose his hand.

"Who are you?" she asked. He paused. That question always jarred him. Every divine creature had multiple names, and he could never remember which of his were still in circulation.

"An angel," he said for the sake of simplicity. "Here to deliver you from evil, and place you into the hands of God."

Her lip curled. "I did not realize that God has such a vested interest in my soul."

"He would not be the only one, it seems." Michael glanced around the room. It still smelled faintly of sulphur. The foul odor lingered like smoke from a pipe, clinging to the walls and curtains and making everything smell ghastly. Young demons could leave their mark for centuries on a house just by walking through the front door. "You can still be set free."

"You are a little late for that," she said. "Thirteen years and five children too late."

"Children?" Michael was brought out of his reverie. He turned his head to give her a long, narrow look.

"Yes," Violet responded. "Who keeps your records? I have five children...or rather, I *had* five. There are only four, now. My eldest son ate the baby and proclaimed her soul a delicacy."

Michael raised his eyebrows. He didn't know how to respond, he was still stuck on 'children'.

Violet shook her head. "Sometimes," she said, "I can hear him through the walls. He moans at night and says his stomach hurts. He wants more."

If she was telling the truth, then there was a greater problem at hand. There was no literature on how to handle demon-born children. It happened so rarely that Michael had begun to doubt their existence. They were sometimes called cambion, and that was all he knew.

He wondered if this woman had any idea of what she had done; of what she had created, suckled, and nurtured into deadly maturity. Any parent in their right mind would have murdered the infant in its cradle. Any Christian woman would have prayed for God to strike her barren before letting one, let alone *five* horrors claw free from her womb.

"I know what you're thinking," she spoke a bit testily when he didn't respond.

"You couldn't possibly."

"You are wondering how I let him do it to me."

Michael shook his head. "It is not my affair." Had decided on that. It was a different department entirely – completely out of his jurisdiction. He had not been sent down here to ponder on the morality of coition between humans and demons. "In any case. No matter what you have done, Heaven still wants you. *God* still wants you and is willing to forgive."

"Is this discussion not better suited for my deathbed?" she asked a bit dryly. "Return in another fifteen or twenty years. We will talk about it then."

Michael furrowed his brow. "I do not think you understand me," he said. "Tonight you are slated to die either way."

Violet felt acid burning in her stomach. She felt like she was going to vomit up her heart into her mouth.

"There is nothing binding you to him," Michael continued. "There is no contract."

Violet's fingers curled inward towards her palm, nails embedding themselves deep into tender flesh. "Of course there is a contract," she said tightly.

"No," Michael pressed, "there was no contract. You signed away your nephew's soul. Do you not remember?"

"I remember," she snarled, "perfectly well."

"Nothing has you bound to Jahangir. *Nothing.*" He reached out to her. His nails were beautifully kept. "If you take my hand, it will all be over."

"I'm sure," she said. "And by that, you mean I will die."

"It will be just as going to sleep," he said softly. "And when you wake up, you will be in paradise."

She hesitated.

"Most people in your position do time for their crimes," he said, wiggling his fingers as if to entice her further. "Signing away your nephew's soul, murdering your sister. It is time done in Purgatory at *least*. This is full-blown once-in-a-lifetime redemption. Offers like this don't just fall from the Savior's lap."

Violet lifted her lady-like hand. It hovered uncertainly over his, fingertips drooping. He could almost touch her. He wanted to reach up, snatch her hand, and drag her back to Heaven if for no other reason than to check this mission off his 'to do' list. Unfortunately, he could not just seize her. Protocol was that she needed to be the one to touch him.

"You are wrong," she said, looking up at him. He resisted the urge to release a very exasperated sigh.

"Angels don't get things wrong," he said. "What is your hesitation? Do you not think you deserve salvation?"

She scoffed. "It is nothing so trite." She pulled her hand away from his entirely. "If someone in Heaven believes I deserve it, then I probably do. Maybe I have done one thing in my life that makes me worthy of redemption or maybe it is just luck of the draw. I will never know. You are wasting your time. I *am* bound to Henry."

"By what?" Michael was now thoroughly agitated.

The look she gave him said every stupid thing he was afraid she would speak out loud.

"You don't understand what is about to happen," he warned. "Jahangir..."

"*Henry.*"

"*Jahangir* is going to crack open your chest and rip out your lungs. He will devour your soul and send it into oblivion. There is no Paradise then; there is no Perdition. There is only eternity and the void."

She was silent.

"He has made himself human to you," Michael said. "I know you cannot see past that. So take my hand and trust me to know what he is capable of – the things he can do to you – you can't even imagine."

Her smile surprised him. It wasn't amused, or even sincere. It was borderline manic. It broke out across her face and she burst out laughing.

"There *are* things he can do. Things *you* can't even imagine." Her hand hovered just outside of her mouth, as if some part of her instinct was to shyly conceal any expression. "Although being an angel, I doubt that you partake."

Michael's eyes narrowed. He clenched his teeth so tightly that a shift of his jaw would have made them squeal. He was suddenly aware of the strongest desire he had ever had to spit in someone's face.

"This is nothing to be made light of," he growled.

Her smile vanished as quickly as it had appeared.

"No one ever said it was," she replied solemnly.

"There are many who devout their entire lives to Heaven and never see its gates."

"I know." She was pressing her finger against the blunt end of her needle, driving it further into the muslin. "I would like to make a request."

"And that would be?"

"Use my space for someone else." She looked back up, meeting his eyes.

He huffed. "Who?"

She did not break eye contact. "My son. Edward."

"Out of the question," Michael responded without hesitation. "His soul is damned, if he even has one. He is half-demon."

"He has a soul. He is half-human as well." She still refused to drop the eye contact, her dark eyes boring straight into his skull. "I cannot force you to do anything, and I don't know how angels work. I know how demons work – I know the quotas they have to fill. I know that one soul is as good as another in the grand scheme of things. And I doubt the Almighty is interested in salvaging my soul specifically. I think He is more interested in keeping as many bodies as possible out of demon clutches. Is that true?"

"More or less," Michael muttered. "In all honesty."

"Then I think the conflict at hand has resolved itself." She finally looked away and leaned further back into her chair. "Take Edward with you instead. He is probably with Claire – in which case, you have the opportunity to claim both. Two previously damned souls plucked out of the mouth of Hell. That won't look too shoddy on your daily report."

Her knowledge of paperwork and how desperately he wished to avoid it made him realize that she had spent far too much time around supernatural beings, and that maybe this was for the best.

He didn't much care anymore. He just wanted to finish the job. Though it was going to be a shame to waste a soul like hers.

"Well," he said. "I don't suppose you know where I can find them?"

It was 3AM, and Drucilla couldn't sleep. Maybe it was because Elliot, despite being the smaller body, managed to take up a considerable amount of space. He had pushed her to the edge until she had been forced to cling to the side, praying that if she were to fall, the softest parts of her would hit the ground first. He had eventually evicted her from the bed altogether. Her options were to attempt to reclaim her spot or move to an empty chair.

Drucilla wrapped her blanket, the one thing she had managed to wrestle free, around her shoulders and started to trail over to the empty chair. The fire had been roaring when they went to bed, but now it was dwindling in its hearth – spitting dim sparks up the chimney. Drucilla adjusted her blanket and sat down in the chair, curling her legs up to tuck her freezing feet underneath her body and trying to arrange herself somewhat comfortably.

She could hear the wood popping. In another fifteen minutes or so it would be completely dead. She would probably want another blanket after that, but she was too lazy to get up and go fetch another one. It would be easier to just freeze.

Drucilla closed her eyes and sighed softly, moving her head to try and find a comfortable resting position. She hadn't quite settled down when she felt a hot sting on her cheek.

Drucilla's forehead crinkled. She reached up to scratch her cheek – feeling another sting on the back of her hand. She opened her eyes and turned to look at the fireplace, a flying spark nearly catching in her eye.

The sparks that had been spiraling up the chimney were now swooping back down and pouring out from the mouth of the fireplace. A few more of them landed on her, catching her nightgown and leaving little black scorch marks wherever they touched. Little red bumps were appearing wherever they touched her hands and face. At this rate, if they didn't stop then Drucilla was going to look like she had contracted the pox.

She stood up, shedding her blanket and she tried to move as quickly as possible out of the range of fire. Heat flushed her face, and she heard the fireplace moan – wheezing like an old man on his deathbed.

An ungodly scraping followed the groan. The new sound was leather and nails, claws dragging over brick. Drucilla didn't know how Elliot was sleeping through it. Her heart started pounding immediately. She backed up so quickly she tripped on the hem of her nightgown; stitches popped and she plummeted face-first to the floor.

Soot was raining down – smothering the embers and blanketing the dim orange glow in grey ash. The log split in half, crumbling to bits as a black leather shoe crashed into its middle.

Drucilla screamed. Black smoke poured from the fireplace, quickly filling up the room. Her eyes filled with tears and her chest clenched with an ugly, hacking cough. She started trying to fight her way to Elliot. She didn't know why he wasn't waking up. He hadn't so much as stirred.

Then the smoke just disappeared. Drucilla looked at the fireplace again, but the shoes had vanished.

"Drucilla," Elliot's voice sounded groggy and annoyed. "What are you screaming about...?"

Drucilla all but ran towards the bed, grabbing at the covers, searching for Elliot's body. Her eyes were still swimming and she could barely see. "Elliot!" She could not pull her voice up above a harsh whisper. "Elliot, we have to leave. We have to leave *now*. James..." She paused. She didn't know why James' name had come to mind, but it felt right. It made sense. She felt her blood start to run a little cold.

"What about James?" Elliot demanded. Drucilla shook her head.

"Not now," she said. "Let me help you up. I'll explain but...trust me when I say we have to leave."

"I'm not going anywhere." Elliot batted her hands away irately. "And what about James?"

Drucilla was starting to feel lightheaded. She drew in a deep breath just so she could feel like she was able to remember how to breathe.

"James is the one we are running from." She felt like she was going to throw up. "I know that doesn't make any sense." She abandoned his bedside and started rummaging around for a trunk or a suitcase...anything would do. She just needed to throw a few of his clothes inside and get him out.

Elliot gripped the covers, running a hand through his messy black hair. It was so thick and oily from sleep. He was in desperate need of a wash. "Is it that time, already?" he asked softly, addressing no one in particular.

"It is three in the morning," she said, not understanding him. A flash of annoyance crossed his face and he pulled himself up into a sitting position, digging his hands into the mattress.

"Leave me alone," he said. "Get out if you want. I don't care where you go."

She paused, staring at him. "Elliot," she said. "I know we have our disagreements. But you do not understand…"

"I understand perfectly well," he snapped. "But you don't know anything about what I have to face. If you were *smart,* you would realize that. And you would run. You wouldn't even stop long enough to look back."

"I don't see how you can do this. I don't see how you can just sit here and wait for something bad to happen. Something…" She couldn't even explain what she thought *might* happen.

"Because it won't stay here if I go. He will hunt me down like a rabbit and break my neck between his teeth. And then you will be caught in the crossfire. Think about it, woman. Have some common sense – some *value* for your own life. You can cover twice as much ground when you're not pushing a man in a wheelchair."

She stared at him for a long time. Her hands were trembling. Her heart would not stop racing. Every inch of her was ready to bolt, and yet she couldn't seem to bring herself to move.

"I can't help but think," she finally said, "that you are just trying to get rid of me."

He threw his hands up in exasperation.

"I tried," he said. "Stay if you will. The world does not need one more fool."

"I am willing to risk my own life for you," she continued to argue. "I don't owe you, I don't even love you. And you snub my efforts."

"If you don't love me, then why bother trying to rescue me?"

"Because no one deserves to be a sitting duck." She was already struggling to dress. The demands of fashion were making a quick flight impossible. She had to abandon the corset, which of course meant that her bodice was a little too snug, and the impression of her nipples against the fabric was borderline obscene.

"In hindsight, maybe I should have warned you."

"Warned me about *what?*" She gave up on trying to adjust her dress and sat down to struggle with stockings and boots. "I'm not going to leave unless it is with you in your chair, Elliot."

A chill ran down Elliot's spine. Acute pain stabbed him in the back, right behind his heart. His blood started racing even as he tried to maintain a cool demeanor. It felt like James was already behind him, slowly reaching for his prize.

His next words were a wet choke. "Drucilla."

She looked at him, alarm written on her face. She had her boot propped up on the edge of a chair, the laces twisted around her fingers.

Elliot shook his head, trying to get his thoughts together. He cleared his throat and tried to breathe through the darting pain. "There is a box on my dresser. Open it."

Drucilla finished tying off her laces then went to do as she was told. She walked quickly up to the dresser where a simple oak box was sitting. She placed her hands against the side and pulled it towards her, opening up the lid and glancing inside. There were only a few things; Elliot's family ring, his cufflinks, a pearl stickpin, and a folding sterling silver pen knife with a mother-of-pearl handle.

"The pen knife should be there," he said.

"It is," she replied.

"Take it. Use it as you need to. It won't do much, but sometimes a few inches in the right place is all it takes."

She looked at him. "But why...?"

"It's just to assuage my own guilt. You should go."

"I am." She pocketed the knife. "Perhaps..." She paused. "In another life...?"

"It's a nice sentiment."

She nodded. She had already wasted more time than she could afford. Without anything further, she left the room.

Elliot closed his eyes and sank back into his pillows.

The darkness was closing in.

CHAPTER 20

"James," Elliot said, his voice barely more than a soft stream of breath. "I know you are there."

The floorboards creaked. Elliot's dug his fingers into the thick bedcovers, gripping the fabric tight.

"You know," his voice was starting to break from the tension. "When you appeared to me for the first time, you tripped on an ottoman."

"And you could not breathe without the aid of a machine." James' voice spread throughout the room. "So much has changed."

"In so little time." Elliot's chest burned. "I didn't think it would be this soon."

"As I said…" James' voice sounded like it was getting fainter. "So much has changed. Including our plans."

Elliot's heart skipped another beat. "James?" There was no response. He sat up a little straighter, pushing himself away from the headboard. Elliot pulled back his covers, leaning over to grab his legs. Elegant hands landed on top of his.

Elliot flinched. He tried to yank his hands back but James held fast, arresting his gaze and staring him down.

"It will hurt a lot less," James said, "if you don't try to resist."

The demon was looming over Elliot, spots of orange starting to bleed through his blue irises. His pupils were getting wider, stretching until they had become cavernous black holes with only a thin ring of blazing color encircling them. His eyes resembled smoldering embers, with bright flecks – like sparks – dancing across their surface.

Every unspoken word was piling up in Elliot's throat, threatening to choke him to death. He could feel his own eyes burning – the pain only getting worse the longer he held onto James' gaze. It felt like someone was trying to dig them out with an unrefined wooden spoon. Blood welled up in the corners, droplets rolling like tears down his high cheekbones and leaving behind faint pink trails.

"I admit..." James trailed his fingers down Elliot's cheek. "I thought you would have more to say." He touched Elliot underneath his chin, fingertips digging into the soft flesh. Suddenly it was like Elliot had swallowed the weight that had been sitting on his tongue. It sprang loose, and he was not in control of what words dribbled from his dry lips.

"Are you feeling generous enough for a last request?" Elliot asked desperately. One of James' clear set of eyelids drooped, slipping up and down his eye distractingly.

"I'm in a giving mood," the demon said.

"Kiss me first." Elliot sounded like he was seventeen again. His voice was weak, trembling. His words reached out searching for a sliver of affection they could hang onto. James' lips parted and he leaned forward, furrowing his brow as he regarded the young lord with nothing less than confusion. The demon tilted his head, the very tip of his pink tongue coming to rest between his white teeth.

"Why?" James asked. Elliot almost burst into tears.

"Does it matter why?" He pulled his hands out of James' slackened grip and rubbed his eyes, spreading blood across his face.

"Yes," James said. "Because I asked."

"I want to know what it feels like."

"To be kissed?"

"To be kissed by *you*, imbecile."

James raised his eyebrows with genuine surprise. He didn't know what he had been expecting. But for some reason, despite Henry's teasing and everyone else's assumptions, he had never truly made the connection...

For a moment, he hesitated. Would it cost so much to humor such a small request? After all, Elliot looked so desperate. It was almost as if simply uttering the request had caused him physical pain. And his lips, which were usually drawn so tight and severe, were more relaxed. Cherry red lips, without any light to give them color, were the color of old blood. James knew that, in an unconventional way, they were enticing. Yet they were unable to draw him in completely.

Still, a kiss. What was one? James allowed himself to lean in even closer, his lips hovering right over Elliot's. James noticed the young lord's throat convulse as he swallowed, lowered eyelids twitching in anticipation.

A single kiss. It could cost him everything. A kiss was affirmation. An indelible stamp of affection pressed into the body's weakest, most vulnerable spot. The lips were a canal straight to the heart. Even a brief touch could give Elliot all he needed.

And what would happen to that ugly, filthy soul when peace settled in, washing away the careful cumulation of piquant hatred and asperity?

James smiled, his lips so close that the movement caused them to brush against Elliot's; the barest of touches.

"Elliot," James said. "If you were at all deserving, don't you think I would have kissed you by now?"

Elliot's eyes opened, and he looked up at James. The demon placed a hand against the lord's chest, skin splitting as thick black claws burst from his nail beds. Elliot's chest was so frail that if he breathed too deeply, his heart could be seen beating. His ribs were as fragile as a child's. James started to apply pressure, and bones began to crack. The thin nightshift offered no resistance to his claws as they ripped open papery skin and parted tender flesh. Elliot screamed while James had the pleasure of sinking his hand into that proud, sickly chest and watch the light ebb from steel grey eyes as a result.

James' pushed his hand into hot, steaming flesh – opening up a large enough hole so that he could slip a second hand in. Elliot's body was convulsing, blood oozing from his mouth. James grabbed hold of the ribcage and cracked it open with disturbingly little effort. Elliot looked like a broken doll on the bed, his head lolling, his dead eyes staring into nothing as his arms, further back now that than they should be, lay motionless at his sides.

James' sleeves were soaked now, wet with blood almost all the way up to the elbow. He started searching for the heart, his fingertips slipping over smooth organs still pulsing for a final grab at life. He found the heart, and he grabbed hold of it, wrenching it free from behind the sternum. He was rewarded by a spray of blood, which hit him in the face and speckled his glasses. James frowned and then set the heart down, putting all of his focus towards the cavity behind it – where Elliot's pitch black soul was nestled.

James opened his mouth, blood mingling and running with saliva as the razor tips of his metal teeth started to pierce through his gums. He didn't know why his teeth were coming up, but he wasn't about to pause and ask questions. The demon grabbed as much of Elliot's soul as he could with one hand; what looked like blackberry jam – some of the balls having burst, the rich juices now adhering the others together. Elliot's soul was so befouled that it had started to rot.

He shoved it all in his mouth. It tasted overwhelmingly like licorice, but with a heavy-handed complexity that was reminiscent of absinthe. One taste, and James lost all control. He grabbed whatever was in his way and shoved it to the side, all the better to push his face down into Elliot's chest cavity, devouring the soul straight from the source without any delicacies in-between. Once or twice James almost choked, he was eating so quickly and the juices were overwhelming. Every fat cluster burst as soon as he closed his mouth around it, gushing down his throat. He licked and gnawed until there was nothing left to devour, and then James pulled back, his stomach already growling and whining for more.

CHAPTER 21

She hadn't touched her embroidery since the angel departed, taking all of her peace and security with him. She had never met one before, but she supposed that was the allure of divine beings. They made their presence addicting before tearing it away, leaving you feeling like a child without its blanket. What better way to bring you to the feet of a deity you could never know otherwise.

Although in retrospect, angels could pick up a trick or two from demons. An angel could control you by your own fears, but a demon baited you with pleasure. Violet had never responded well to intimidation, but she was a fool for her vices.

"Violet."

She hadn't even heard the door open.

"Henry." She pushed her embroidery off her lap, tossing it into the basket beside her chair.

"Did you know our children are missing?"

Violet released a breath she didn't know she had been holding. "You were looking for them?"

"I visited their room. All I saw was one of the maids. She was lying in a pool of her own blood and her eyes had been ripped out from her sockets." Henry stopped just behind her chair, reaching down to settle his hands on her shoulders. "You wouldn't know anything about that?"

Violet stood. She turned to face him, wondering if her terror was written out on her face.

He still didn't look like a demon. He was leaning against the chair, one ankle hooked around the other, mildly annoyed.

He looked like her husband.

"Something tells me," he kept his voice low and dark as he spoke, "that there is no prelude to this nocturne."

"I've played it over in my head," she responded softly. "I never could settle on how it began. Or ended."

"We both know how this will end." He abandoned the chair and started to move towards her. "Are you going to fight it?"

She tilted her chin up. "Do you expect me to fight?"

"The woman I married does not buck against the inevitable." He slid a hand over her hair where it was pulled tight back, away from her face. "She always faces defeat with grace."

"The woman you married is not the woman who stayed with you," she told him. "The woman you married wasn't a fool."

He laughed. "Are you saying the years have dulled your edge?"

"I'm saying of all my bad decisions, you are the one that haunts me still."

"Oh, that hurts." He rested a hand against his chest. "I like to think I am not your worst decision. After all, you could have stayed married to your first husband."

"I would not have lasted another thirteen years with him."

"And you would have been another boring, dutiful wife giving in to consumption."

"We have children together."

"I have already apologized for that."

"I don't want..." She closed her eyes, swallowing the lump that was making her throat ache. "I don't want it to end like this."

He seemed slightly surprised. He brushed his fingers over the curve of her cheek, trailing his nails down her neck. "You're scared?"

She nodded. "Do you hate me for admitting it?"

"Disappointed, perhaps." He leaned forward and pressed his lips to her cheek. "And yet flattered."

"I love you," she whispered, placing a hand on the back of his head and keeping her lips close to his. "Surely it does not *have* to end here?"

He hesitated, settling a hand on her waist.

"We were made for each other." Her voice sounded strained. "Made for eternity. Henry, people like us do not collide bodies by mistake."

And there was the disconnect. *People. Bodies.* Neither of those words meant anything to him. This skin he was wearing was not his own. It was a deception.

Yet he could not deny there was something. He felt it whenever he touched her waist, or whenever she fell asleep beside him – her head tucked into his shoulder. He had felt it again when he held their eldest son for the first time, and all of their babies after that…

Henry pulled her a little closer. She gasped and rested her head against his chest, clinging to him, inhaling the faint traces of cologne that still clung to his shirt. He dropped a kiss onto her hair, and she tilted her head back, catching the next one with her lips.

The power behind her kiss was as fierce as ever, but he could not pull his attention away from her tired posture, the way she was leaning against him. She was worn down, she was letting her emotions show as a final defense, because she could not claw her way out of this one.

Thirteen years. A long time, and getting older every day.

People. Bodies. It wasn't meant to last.

Henry pulled his head back. She looked up at him, her lips still slightly parted and red. He held her gaze and placed two of his fingers against her bottom lip. Violet closed her mouth around his fingers and started sucking on them, moaning a little as he started to move them back and forth, slipping them over her tongue.

Henry pushed her up against the wall, shoving his fingers even deeper inside. Violet let out a sound of surprise but opened her mouth wider to accommodate. Henry watched her – the way her hands held onto his wrist. That feeling was back, tightening like a band around his stomach.

Love? Perhaps.

Yet dangerously close to hunger pangs.

Henry started pushing more of his hand into her mouth. Violet scrunched up her brow, making a sound of protest as he fit more of his fingers inside, followed by his knuckles. He kept going, even though her jaw was stretched to the maximum. The back of his hand grazed against her teeth, and Violet's screams were muffled as the corners of her mouth split apart. Her cheeks ripped open, giving her a grotesque smile from ear-to-ear. She thrashed, gagging, trying to scream as Henry held on to the small of her back, keeping her pinned between him and the wall. He kept reaching down her throat, focusing on the prize. He didn't even notice when she stopped moving.

His hands found her heart. He impatiently reached behind it, grabbing hold of the little pocket that contained her soul. He closed his fist around it and dragged it back up through her throat, letting her ruined body slump against the wall and slide down to the floor. Henry held the wet meat in his hands, small enough to fit into his palm. He swiped away the blood and slid his nail down the front, opening it up enough so that he could see what was inside.

Henry smiled and held it high above his head, squeezing the contents out into his mouth. He stuck out his tongue and Violet's silver soul slipped down his throat, breaking against the sharp little points of metal that were starting to protrude from his gums. The juices flowed, the sharp, bitter taste making his whole body shudder. Henry moaned and finally put the whole thing in his mouth, sucking it dry, dragging it between his teeth to make sure he got every precious morsel before swallowing.

CHAPTER 22

The house was nearly empty. The servants, having caught wind of trouble long before anyone else, had already hidden or fled. Drucilla picked her way through an abandoned kitchen, both of her hands out in front of her as she tried not to run into anything solid.

She had decided halfway down the stairs that the servant's entrance would be her best chance of escape. She was nearly there, and from that point she would have to figure out how to reach the city...

Movement. Drucilla froze, her hand dropping down into her skirt's pocket to find the little silver penknife. She didn't say anything, she just stood there and waited to see if she was being followed or if she had simply been spooked by a draft.

More movement – followed by the awkward clanking of a bell. Drucilla squinted, her eyes having adjusted enough to the darkness that she could make out the details of the thing that was approaching her.

It looked like a man – but the skinniest man she had ever seen. He was dragging himself across the floor, crawling, his jutting ribcage scraping the ground. His matted hair hung in limp, dirty tendrils around his shoulders and a leather collar hung loose and heavy around his red, chaffed neck. The bell clanked dolefully with each rise and fall of his shoulders. It seemed to take him an eternity to cross the room – apparently he had been sleeping behind the stove; what would have been a luxury for a naked body covered in gaping sores.

He looked up at her. His eyes were rimmed with red and weeping. His bottom lip was so dry it had split open, and his whole chin was caked with dried blood. He looked like he was trying to speak, but the only sound coming out was a dry rattle.

Drucilla tightened her grip on the small knife, more repulsed by the disgusting creature than threatened. She started to lower herself down into a crouch, morbid curiosity getting the better of her as she extended a hand.

The man didn't move. She got a little closer, resting her hand against his cheek. He cringed but didn't pull away, his arms trembling with exertion and the effort of holding himself up.

"There," she said softly. "You're not a threat to anyone, are you?"

He leaned into her hand. His cheek was grimy, and the very act of touching him made her skin crawl. Drucilla kept turning the penknife around in her free hand. She couldn't imagine what life must be like for this thing. She wondered if he retained any memories from the life he lived before he had everything taken from him. She wondered if he had ever *been* human, or if this was just some sort of dark, twisted illusion…

No, maybe not that. It felt too real to just be her imagination. Still, she couldn't leave him down here. If James came after her, once he was through with Elliot, then he would surely cross paths with this thing and then it would be done for…

But then again, she couldn't just take this creature with her. He'd just slow her down.

Drucilla wanted to jerk her hand back – away from oily, dirty skin and harsh stubble. She was frozen to in place. The hand resting against his cheek was trembling, fingers twitching. She couldn't walk away from him, but she couldn't be his caretaker either.

Elliot had been her first failure. It was just all going to slide downhill from there.

Drucilla got a grip on her penknife, closing her soft hand around it. She hesitated only a second more before looping fingers through his collar, tugging the tortured thing closer before pressing the very tip of the knife against his neck.

The man whimpered and tried to back away, bowing his head and hunching his shoulders like a cowed dog. Drucilla snarled disdainfully, clenching her teeth in determination as she drove the tip deeper, and dark blood welled to the surface. She had to angle the knife, digging underneath his collar. He yelped, and she started sawing, dragging the blade across his throat. It was neither big enough nor sharp enough to slit him open like she wanted, but it was getting the job done.

He choked, gargling his own blood. Ragged flaps of skin moved with his desperate gasps that were now being pulled through the ghastly opening in his throat. His leather collar was soaked with blood. It streamed down his neck, pooling in the hollows of his collarbone.

It ended when Drucilla jammed the blade so deeply into his neck that it lodged inside and stuck fast. She couldn't pull it out again easily, especially not with her hand coated in blood as it was. She wasn't about to sit and wrestle him for it, either. Best to just leave it.

Drucilla leaned back and placed her hands against the floor, drawing up her knees to scrabble backwards. The hem of her dove grey dress was now stained dark maroon. In the surrounding darkness, the blood looked almost black.

His body was still twitching. The blood was gushing like water from a cracked porcelain bowl.

She had to leave. She had to get out of here.

Drucilla pushed herself up onto her feet, gathering her skirt up in her bloody hands. She left rust-colored streaks on whatever she touched as she fled, bolting out the servant's entrance without another hesitant thought.

Henry sat on the steps that led up to his townhouse, his hands restlessly fiddling with his cufflinks. Clouds were rumbling overhead. Enormous grey sentinels, heavy and severe, reflected his mood perfectly with their grumbles and threats of miserable weather.

"Why aren't you inside?”

Henry did not look up, not even when he heard the scuffle of James' shoes as they made their swift ascent.

"I was waiting on you," Henry responded, picking at a loose thread on his crisp, folded white cuff.

James snorted. "It is *your* house Henry. You have a key."

Henry made a face and tugged on the thread, snapping it. "I felt like waiting. Was it only Elliot?"

"Only Elliot. His wife left and I did not bother pursuing."

"I could not find my two children."

"Well, you have two more."

Henry looked up, his pupils narrowing as they caught the light. "I do…oh for the love of God." He sighed. "I had forgotten." He looked at the townhouse behind him. "I could have taken care of them by now. I feel as though we've already lingered too long. We should just go."

"I don't think it would be advisable to leave them alive," James said. "You can't help having lost the other two. But you should tie up as many loose ends as possible."

"You're right," Henry said. He stood, brushing off the knees of his trousers. "I am ready to put this behind us. But you know, I have to ask…"

James adjusted his glasses. "It was well worth it."

Henry flashed him a grin. "Hers, too."

He opened up the front door and stepped inside, James following closely at his heels.

There was a strange smell. It hit them full-force as soon as they walked through the door. James gagged, putting his hand over his mouth and nose. It smelled like blood, or money – two scents nearly indistinguishable from one another. Underneath it was a slightly more sour scent – the beginnings of decay.

"Someone got here before we did," James whispered, putting Henry instantly on edge.

"And now the question begs who – and are they still here?" Henry took another step forward. The smooth sole of his shoe slipped and his leg jerked, nearly pitching him backward. Henry fought to regain his balance, grabbing onto James' shoulder. He looked down at the floor, chest heaving as he tried to catch his breath.

Oil. Whale oil. There was a thick trail of it straight across the floor, leading to the staircase the vanished into the upper level.

Henry glanced at James and then started making his way closer to the stairs, treading with more care the second time around. James felt the fine hairs on the back of his neck prickle, his skin tingling with each step.

"Satan?" James hissed, hazarding a guess.

"I doubt it. We would be mincemeat."

"We've just barely stepped through the door."

"My point exactly. We would not have made it this far."

James rolled his eyes. The sour smell was getting stronger, almost overpowering the heavy copper stench.

There was a loud thud and something crashed at the top of the stairs. A flash of white, and then a body started careening down the stairs, looking like a doll that had been thrown. It hit the edge of every other step, bouncing grotesquely until it landed at the bottom with a ghastly crunch.

The body was mangled. Every limb was twisted in the wrong direction, an insect that someone had stepped on.

Henry sighed and pinched the bridge of his nose. "The nursemaid."

James looked up. The top of the stairs was enshrined in blackness. He lowered one of his clear eyelids, the colors of mortal earth fading to grey around him. In the very center of the darkness, he could see her sickly skin, a shade of green so murky that it almost looked grey. Thick black oil dripped from her long, tapered fingertips and the ends of her hair trailed off into tendrils of fetid smoke.

When he slid the lid back again, she was walking down the stairs – peeling back the darkness like a curtain to reveal the beautiful feminine form that Greed had always favored when sealing herself inside mortal flesh.

"It is about time." She had a voice like an abrupt memo, or a sharp note signed by the management. "I didn't think you two were ever going to arrive."

"It didn't occur to you to look for us yourself?" Henry asked. He hadn't moved. His shoulders were stiff, but his thumbs were hooked in his pockets, appearing relaxed.

"I knew you would come back here," Greed said. "You left behind too many loose ends."

"Well, only two," Henry replied flippantly. "And they're gone now, aren't they? Did you eat their souls?"

Greed tilted her head. "I ate them whole," she said. "I opened my mouth and swallowed their lives and bones."

"Better than any demon." Henry flashed a grin. "That's why you run your own department."

Greed narrowed her eyes. "Don't make me kill you, Jahangir."

"Oh, that's not why you're here?" Henry glanced at James from the corner of his eye.

"No. I'm here to drag you down to Hell and let Satan be the one to do the honors."

"See, it's a damned shame. And I don't mean that in jest." Henry lifted his hands defensively. "I mean, shouldn't you be looking for Meriwether? This is *his* clerical error after all."

"He and I have an arrangement," Greed said. "Unfortunately, the only thing it guaranteed was that he would have the chance to warn you. It doesn't appear that he was counting on you being a ripe pair of fools."

"No..." James rubbed his chin. "He was probably banking on it."

Henry was trying to maintain his composure while looking wildly around the hallway, searching for anything he could use to aid their escape. All he could see were the countless lamps that the servants kept lit. Bright, blazing lamps that had drawn him to Violet in the first place. A moth to a candle...

He glanced at Greed again. She would go up in flames faster than an oil-soaked rag. Too fast to escape her meat. A single lamp was all he needed. The floor was already coated in oil. But nothing was within his reach, and if he moved, she would take him down in the span of a heartbeat.

Greed stepped over the dead nursemaid. The closer she got, the more Henry could feel his flesh quiver. It was as if his whole body was ready to split apart and dissolve. His hands were shaking uncontrollably. He couldn't keep them in his pockets anymore. He felt like hot needles were being driven into his raw nailbeds as long, curling black talons began to sprout from his fingertips. Henry closed his eyes, squeezing out black, acidic blood from the corners. It stung, burning a trail down his cheeks. He could feel it eating away at his skin, his eyes. His clear eyelids slipped down for protection, all three at once, the colors of mortal earth vanishing with dizzying speed. Now the main focus was the Sin in front of him, having gone from sultry to insidious within a matter of seconds. She had a wide, grotesque grin that split her face open; and so many sharp metal teeth.

She was close enough to touch him, now. She was sliding her hands over his cheeks, resting them against his neck, her thumbs against the hinges of his jaw. His own metal teeth were splitting open his gums, piercing through his lips when they could not escape quickly enough. Henry opened his mouth, and the flesh ripped, blood pouring down his throat as his body was being ruined by the emerging demonic form.

She was going to force it out of him. She was going to make him change. And when he had ripped away the last scrap of human flesh, she was going to do the same to James and drag them both back down to hell.

"Jahangir the Conqueror." She opened her mouth, and her split tongue licked the blood away from his face, burning away more flesh wherever it trailed. "Mojgan the Bright."

James felt like his bowels were being spooned out. His stomach clenched and he doubled over, gagging and dry-retching. His stomach heaved again, and he coughed, feeling like he had been stabbed in the lungs. He felt like there was something lingering at the back of his throat, like a hair, or something else he couldn't quite reach. James opened his mouth wide and pushed his fingers as far back as he could, making himself choke. He retched again, and this time something came up. Yellow bile spewed from his mouth, and a whole fistful of squirming white maggots.

James felt the blood drain from his face. He glanced back up, his glasses slipping down his sweaty skin. He could see what Greed was doing to Henry, though he was fighting the change with every last bit of strength he had in his reserve. She was going to win. Something had to be done.

James vomited again, more maggots and bile pouring out of his mouth. He gasped and shuddered, wiping his mouth with the back of his hand as he kept his head down and crept away, backing up as much as he could. He knew if he moved too suddenly, she would turn her attack on him. But right now she was focused, and her effort showed. Henry was closer to being Jahangir with each passing second.

His heel hit something wood. James glanced behind him to see that he had run into a shelf. He all but had his back up against the wall, and now he was surrounded by a dozen whale oil lamps.

James looked at the lamps, then back at the floor. It was still shiny with oil. Greed must have bathed the place with it, perhaps some sort of baptismal rite – a tribute to the fallen family's avarice.

Whatever. James reached out and grabbed one of the lamps. He didn't know if the entire floor had been washed with oil or if there were only spots, but he did not have time to speculate. He flung the lamp as far as he could, and he heard it crash. But he was already grabbing another, using both hands to throw whichever lamps were closest to him.

They broke as soon as they hit the ground, and their quivering flames lapped up the oil hungrily. Sparks danced across the pools, making black pockmarks on Greed's smooth legs. And that was all it took.

She screamed, but the noise was drowned out by the roar of a rushing fire. She was engulfed from top to bottom so quickly that James almost didn't register what was happening. She staggered back, slipping on the floor and crashing to the ground. Her face was melting like wax, the smell absolutely putrid. It was more than a burning corpse, it was like burning a corpse that had already been dead for weeks.

James raced across the room, focusing first on not slipping and busting open his face. He grabbed Henry when he was close enough, gripping fistfuls of the other demon's shirt by the shoulders and all but dragging him out, headed for the front door. The flames had developed a life of their own, and they were set to destroy anything in their path. The house was lost. The whole black, bloody business was about to be nothing but ashes.

James all but threw Henry down the front steps. The two demons collapsed onto the sidewalk, bloody heaps of shredded skin and fine clothes. Henry's demon form was already retreating. His eyes were back to normal, and his teeth had completely vanished. He reached up with one gory hand and his jaw cracked as he set it back into place.

"Are you all right?" James asked, gasping.

Henry nodded, moving his jaw a little bit to work out the kinks before responding verbally. "We're screwed."

"We just made things infinitely worse for ourselves," James agreed. "Once Greed gets back to Hell…"

"It will be a long time before she can get another flesh form. Centuries, probably."

"They will send someone else before that," James said. "Or Satan Himself will see fit…"

He let that idea hang. They sat in solemn silence, watching the fire eat the house from the inside out.

"Where are we going next?" Henry finally asked. "Do we follow Lady?"

"I haven't the foggiest where he is. We will just have to try our luck and see where we land."

"We don't have any luck." Henry snorted. "We're going to end up with our heads in baskets."

"It is better than Hell," James said, already starting to stand up.

"Yes, well." Henry was still seated, not quite ready to move. "I suppose anything is."

JASPER BLACK

Jasper Black is the author of the *Swallow You Whole* series and lives in North Carolina with his wife, their child, and his other partners.

His biggest inspirations are Judeo-Christian mythology and the artwork of Yana Toboso. When he isn't writing, he squabbles with the resident demons and organizes his bookshelf.